OBAMA
ON
EDGE

CREATIVE EXPRESSIONS
FROM A HISTORIC TIME

George Thomas Clark

Published by GeorgeThomasClark.com

ISBN: 978-1-7332981-2-4 – Trade Paperback
Copyright 2019 by George Thomas Clark

GeorgeThomasClark.com
Bakersfield, California
webmaster@GeorgeThomasClark.com

Books by George Thomas Clark

Hitler Here
Trump Time
The Bold Investor
Paint it Blue
Basketball and Football
Death in the Ring
Tales of Romance
In Other Hands
Echoes from Saddam Hussein
Obama on Edge

Acknowledgements

Barack Obama's first autobiography, "Dreams from My Father," provides much essential and entertaining information about his family history. Smithsonian, The New Yorker, The Atlantic, Rolling Stone, The Los Angeles Times, Al Jazeera, The Christian Science Monitor, Bakersfield.com, The Texas Tribune, Wikipedia, AllVoices.com, and RickPerry.com also have helpful articles.

Introduction

In these satirical columns written from 2007 to 2012, Barack Obama's African grandfather espouses pride and aggressive self-defense. His father discusses academic success, family difficulties, and a tragic drinking problem. Young Obama reveals his struggle to control vices and establish racial identity. Then the soaring young politician offers incisive comments about politics, international relations, the media, and other issues. A variety of adversaries counterattack. Sarah Palin, Sean Hannity, and Rush Limbaugh claim they are appalled by Obama. John McCain bemoans that the young man lacks an understanding of big league politics. Hillary Clinton doubts his American values. Jeremiah Wright insists Obama always knew what his pastor was preaching and why. Mahmoud Ahmadenijad presumes to lecture the new president. Mitt Romney thinks Obama is a loser. Osama bin Laden, Muammar Gaddafi, and Bashar al-Assad also disapprove. These characters and others have a pulpit. They want *Obama on Edge*.

Contents

Prologue

2009-2011

2012

PROLOGUE

CHAPTER 1

Grandfather of Obama

Villagers often said I had ants in my anus but that no more bothered me than their saying hello. They were simple people, uneducated and without ambition, and I was proud to be different learning to read and write, eating with knives and forks, and bathing twice daily. White men paid me to cook in their houses, and I saved wages to invest in cattle. Back home, I demanded my hut be immaculate. If one of my girlfriends failed to thoroughly clean or broke something, I beat her. She had to understand. I was Onyango Obama, a serious and temperate man.

I waited long to get married and then was patient with my wife Helima despite her barrenness. She knew the problem could not have been mine. I was a strong man dancing as I looked for another woman in a hall in Nairobi and not worried about bumping into people or stepping on toes. A loudmouth shouldn't have said I was already an old man with a wife and cattle but no children and must therefore have a problem between my legs. I hit him with my right fist then another right and left and kicked him in the groin and jumped on his fallen flesh and pummeled till I was pulled off.

I would've gone back to the village anyway. I needed a beautiful young woman and investigated all. The best was Akumu but her father had already committed her to another man and received six cattle. I said send those back and I'll give you fifteen this minute. He agreed, and the following morning my friends performed the ceremonial capture of Akumu and carried her kicking happily to my hut where Helima ran off to stay with neighbors while I made Akumu my wife and soon had a daughter, Sarah, and a son, Barack, and took a fresh sixteen-year old, also named Sarah, as my third wife and kept her in Nairobi where I worked for a white man who tried to strike me with a cane I blocked and snatched away to cane his hateful hide.

That is an example why Christianity, which I had tried, repulsed me. Christ was weak and so was his doctrine of forgiveness. I doubted white men really believed in all that. Like ants white men worked together and built their businesses and nations, unlike foolish black men who will always lose. Thankfully, I by nature possessed iron discipline and a clenched fist. My newest wife understood she needed beatings to

3

keep her in line. All women should have deferred, but Akumu often complained and twice deserted her children and me and each time I marched to her father's village to demand her return which he granted.

When World War II began I ordered my wives to behave while I served in British regiments as a cook. Among other places I traveled to Arabia, Ceylon, and Burma where I obtained a fourth wife delighted to belong to a strong man of fifty. She stayed there and I returned to Kenya and found Helima unwilling to move to a village with land favorable to crops I'd learned to grow. That didn't bother me long. She was old as I was. Akumu and Sarah came with me and watched my bananas and mangoes cover the horizon and bring money along with cattle I sold to build each of them a hut and one for myself.

Sarah bore two children and behaved while Akumu repeatedly disrespected me and had to be thrashed but still failed to complete chores, forcing me to be sterner still. When my daughter Sarah was twelve and Barack nine, Akumu kidnapped our third child, an infant, and in the night rushed to her family's village. I didn't want her back but she had abandoned two children. After two weeks of consideration, I confronted her family and learned they'd already accepted a dowry from a man she'd married and accompanied to Tanganyika. Akumu was in fact so treacherous and irresponsible she told our daughter Sarah to wait a few weeks then take Barack and walk through wilderness to her parents' village. Two weeks later, I found them starving, thirsty, mauled by insects, and covered with dirt. I broke down, but only briefly, and then fed and cleaned them up and took them back to my wife Sarah with news they were now hers.

Daughter Sarah was bright and would probably marry well and did not need the money for schooling I gave Barack, whom I had long tutored in reading and mathematics. Sometimes teachers caned my intelligent son for correcting them in class. A few years later he became one of the elite young African students in Kenya, earning admission to a mission secondary school fifty miles away. He received good grades but secretly took girls to his dormitory and stole chickens and crops from neighboring farms and shamed me when he was expelled and for that I caned his back till it bled.

Father of Obama

Dear Barry,

I'm most proud of you but naturally grieve as I read how you feel about me. Please understand, in many respects I enjoy your book, and do not here write so much to refute, which perhaps I could not honestly do anyway, but to explain. You did not grow up in an African village, and Onyango Obama was not your father but mine. He was a bright and ambitious man but of another world in which strong, respected men beat their wives and children. Imagine if I, or anyone else, had done this to you. Would you still be so gentle and stable, as I confidently state you are? Let your father surmise you'd be more like me.

Last time the old man battered me I considered grabbing the cane and turning it on him. Fortunately, I didn't, and though he banned me from his compound he got me a job as a clerk over on the coast in Mombasa. You're correct, I didn't stay long, and doubt you would have, either. The Arab owner upbraided me every day and after a fortnight I stood almost on his toes and said not another word and then left without pay. Scurrying to obtain another job, I settled for paltry wages but, on a visit, told my father I in fact earned more. He demanded to see a pay book he knew I couldn't produce and banned me again before storming into his hut.

Did you have to pay to marry your wife? You know I did, not with money but soul as Father kept rejecting my request to provide a dowry for Kezia's parents. I then had to ask her to intercede, and only that – the logic and appeal of my beautiful girlfriend – compelled hard Obama to accept that a man with assets should help his son procure a bride. What an oppressive existence I then entered. Did I, like you, easily matriculate to Occidental College and then Columbia University? You, my at times self-righteous son, should've juxtaposed our experiences. I had to bow to become an office boy. Meanwhile, my less bright friends were going to universities and preparing for lives of affluence.

I loved my wife and infant son but they were suffocating me.

5

You, as a young adult, were free to study and roam. I worked all day and studied correspondence courses during breaks and hours every night, striving to qualify for an American university. Ultimately, I took the tests. Results wouldn't arrive for months I spent losing weight, grinding inside about the prisoner I'd be if I failed. I couldn't fail. I wouldn't. I didn't. With glee I shouted after my acceptance. My father now appreciated me but lacked the means for this. How would I pay? You're quite lucky, indeed more so than I, that the University of Hawaii, wherever that was, offered me a scholarship I embraced before saying goodbye to little Roy and my pregnant wife.

I had to get a good education and worked quite hard. My social life came rather more readily as I'd always been a charmer. Right away I met a white teenager, Ann, and knew she wanted me. I probably didn't explain all the complexities of my domestic life in Kenya but that didn't matter now in Hawaii. Soon, in 1961, we married, and you were born a few months later when she was eighteen. I was already twenty-five, and two years later received my economics degree. Please understand, I would have liked – or at least had no overriding objection to – living with you and your mother. But to do so I would've had to accept a comprehensive scholarship from the rather mundane New School in New York City and reject academically elite Harvard, which offered only tuition. My son, I fear I had to lovingly leave another family. Under the same circumstances, can you swear you wouldn't have done the same? Your response, though of emotional interest, is not relevant to the decision I inexorably made in 1963.

I must tell you, and I don't believe it immodest, that the ladies loved me at Harvard as in Hawaii and Kenya. After I got my masters degree in economics, a most determined Ruth chased me back home and insisted we marry. I agreed. That was reasonable. Your mother had divorced me. And Kezia understood the rules: Roy and Auma came to live with Ruth and me and that arrangement was satisfactory until Ruth and I had two sons, Mark and David, and she began nurturing hers and rejecting mine. That's not why I drank, of course. I simply loved getting loaded on the finest whiskey and cigarettes, while wearing the most elegant suits, and frequenting the most fashionable hotels, restaurants, and nightclubs. If one drink felt good, why would I quit?

At work I presided over economic policy at important corporations and ministries but began to be required to train buffoons who'd been promoted over me because of tribal biases in government. This enraged me, as you've written, since it showed Kenyan politicians had simply replaced white colonialists. Friends said keep quiet. Even sober I wouldn't do that, and after drinks in public I'd bellow a Harvard man of great training and insight should not be so mistreated. Our great President Jomo Kenyatta, a champion of maiming clitorises, ordered me into his office and said there'd be no shoes on my feet by the time I got another job. I was banned, blacklisted, shorn of my passport and in every way humiliated until forced to take a job far beneath me.

Ruth, get up at once, I'd shout walking in late at night. I'm hungry. Cook me this and that. To Roy and Auma I offered many a rebuke. They needed to be disciplined. Because of my attainments, all Obamas had to be number one. And my whole family needed to give me the respect my nation denied. I should have had a chauffeur. That would've helped after I left the nightclub. I don't recall much, really. I woke up maimed in the hospital and tormented by news I'd killed a white farmer. I know you visited Ruth and heard all this and her claims I was crazy and Mark's that I was a drunk unavailable to him. What I'm describing is something other than insanity, though a year in the hospital made me pray for peace.

Soon after release, I didn't mind, that is I didn't implode, when Ruth left with Mark and David and filed for divorce. I still had Roy and Auma with me, and two new sons, Bernard and Abo, out in the village with Kezia. And I had you in Hawaii. There I journeyed in December 1971 when you were ten. In your book I learn you'd told friends I was a prince. Instead, you met a convalescing man who'd just made a grueling trip half way around the globe. My hug you greeted with arms pinned to your sides.

I understand you're doing very well in school, I said. You didn't respond so I commented intelligence was in our blood and that your brothers and sister in Africa also excelled in school. I wasn't shy as a boy but you decidedly were, and more than twenty years later in writing you reveal why: as I talked to Ann and her parents, who were raising you, you stared at me and concluded I was strikingly thin and had bony knees cutting into the legs of my pants and carried an ivory-handled cane since I walked with a limp and exuded a fragility that haunted you as much as the yellow of my malarial eyes. In your book you're satisfied to merely note I'd been badly injured in an automobile accident, not that I had in fact had lost both legs and ached like hell forevermore. My son, let other people write that. You feel it more important to declare you were tired of me after a week and preferred fantasies you could "alter" and that would wall off the "volatile and vaguely threatening" man in your living room.

You did have some bad habits. Most disturbing, you watched too much television. One night I told you to go to your room, overruling your grandmother's suggestion you simply watch the Christmas season cartoon in there, and explained if you've finished your lesson for tomorrow then begin work for the next day and if you've already done that then start the lessons you'll have after vacation and do so before you make me angry. You sulked into your room and listened to your grandmother call me a bully and grandfather remind me this was his house. And you'd already heard him complain I was sitting in his chair and her snap she wasn't my servant. Though you were "counting the days until I left," I'm glad you acknowledge being proud I riveted your teacher and classmates with a lecture about evolution and wild animals and tribes and slavery and that "Kenyans, like all of us in the room, longed to be free and develop themselves through hard work and sacrifice."

I wish you'd known I asked your mother to bring you to live with me in Kenya. You would've joined Roy and Auma, who were most delighted by the idea, and been part of a big happy family. But Ann felt my life was too complicated, and she was ever allured by Indonesia, even after divorcing her husband from there.

You're undoubtedly fortunate not to have come. I lost my lousy job and had to take Roy and Auma to live in a ramshackle house in a ghetto. Despite being one of the brightest and most capable men in the country, I borrowed money for food while many people I'd given aid shunned me. Hell with them. In bars other fellows seemed fine after I'd downed sufficient whiskey. I suppose liquor always made me hungry, for your sister is honest, as you write, that I'd stagger in quite late and burst into her bedroom and say get me something to eat right now, quit frowning, talk to me. Roy couldn't stand me and had already left home, and Auma prayed I'd never return. She didn't have to see me much after a scholarship enabled her to board at Kenya High School.

Eventually I was readmitted to government, albeit at a too low level, but decided not to burden myself with home ownership and instead resided in undistinguished hotels where I could bring my young girlfriends. When one complained about my nightlife, I replaced her. They weren't going to stop me from having a fine time. No one could till the night I smashed into something and never woke up.

You write your mother cried over the phone when you told her but you, Barry, felt no pain nor any reason to pretend so. I understand and for that reason am especially gratified as a young man you left your vacation in Europe, feeling it was a place not your own, and embraced Africa where, eloquently, you remember everywhere feeling and seeing and smelling my presence, and out in the village, under the enduring mango tree, you knelt at my grave and that of my father, and for all of us you cried.

Sincerely,

Your Father

Billie Holiday Visits Young Obama

I love cigarettes smoking my head with an odor beer washes away until I smoke more then get down with whiskey and mellow more with reefer before a little blow rushes my brain then crashes me alone after a party in an apartment echoing above with other empty people. I don't care I'm not white but concerned if I'm really black enough, a high school senior in Honolulu maybe no one will accept so I'm angry and resentful and pour more drinks to relax and spend another night with Billie Holiday.

I know the trick is not caring it hurts when I put out matches with my fingers but understand Billie feels more since to survive she needs smack I avoid with visions of a needle-launched bubble racing through veins to stop my heart. The wheel of fortune never stops for Billie I embrace like a lover, saddened and soothed by her sweet lament it's so easy to remember but so hard to forget.

2008

CHAPTER 2

High-Riding Hillary Stomps Obama

A couple thousand cowboys, drifters, hookers, and horses had surrounded the Philadelphia Saloon near the Liberty Bell last Wednesday night. They were a raucous and happy group because their candidate, Hillary Clinton, had just trounced Barack Obama in a showdown debate, bolstering her chances for victory in the presidential primary April twenty-second and suggesting her tidal wave from Ohio and Texas will also sweep through this state all the way to Pennsylvania Avenue. I wanted to enter the establishment but was frankly afraid to try. Thankfully, one of Hillary's crack media consultants lassoed me and pulled me inside and, with a kick to my fanny, propelled me toward the candidate, who was standing at the bar.

"Line 'em up," Hillary ordered the bartender. He complied, placing six shot glasses of whiskey on the bar. With her right hand she grabbed the one on that end and chugged it, then used her left to finish that shot – right, left, right, left – and all were gone, and Hillary kicked the wooden side of the bar, spat on the floor, yelled "Fuckin', yeah," and with rapidity likely to win any showdown she drew the gun on her right hip and fired three shots into the ceiling and on a finger twirled her gun before re-holstering it. Inside and out, everyone roared, and that included me.

"Madame President," said campaign chief George Stephanopoulous, "will you please grant this tinhorn a few minutes? He has an international readership."

"I reckon so," said Hillary, offering her hand and almost breaking mine.

"Senator Clinton, Barack Obama had been enchanting millions of Americans until tonight," I said. "What was the key to your damaging that relationship?"

"The man's a cotton-pickin' elitist," she said. "He's way out of touch with middle America. What kind of high horse is he on, saying that small-town Americans bitter about hard times 'cling to guns or religion or antipathy to people who aren't like them.' If I weren't a lady, I'd beat his ass. He should realize these people have been around guns all their lives, just like I've been since the morning my daddy put a revolver instead of a rattler in my crib. For centuries these Americans have hunted together because they needed the food, and even the ones who didn't need bloody meat cherished the bonding that comes from the chase and the kill. A guy like Barack Hussein Obama could never understand that."

"Respectfully, Senator Clinton, given that you and your husband have made more than a hundred million bucks during the last seven years, isn't it hypocritical to call him elitist?"

My heart stabbed when Mrs. Clinton stroked her gun but she quickly thrust her right index finger into my face and fired, "I'm rooted in middle class values. They are the heart and soul of the American experience. Maybe my opponent doesn't have the background to understand that."

"Are you implying that Senator Obama isn't thoroughly American?"

"I didn't say that. But I'm glad you did. Look at his associations. His pastor, Jeremiah Wright, wants God to damn America. And he's a crony of Bill Ayers, the 1970's terrorist from the Weather Underground that bombed government buildings and killed police."

"Ayers didn't participate in the crimes you mention," I said. "He was in hiding. When he emerged, he didn't have to serve jail time because of 'government legal misconduct.' Your husband, President Clinton, pardoned two fellow members of the Weather Underground, Linda Sue Evans, who drove the getaway car from a robbery during which three were killed, including two police officers, and the other, Susan Rosenberg, who was caught with more than seven hundred pounds of dynamite. What do you say to that?"

"There's a difference big as Texas, and this is it: the two ladies my husband pardoned are repentant and Bill Ayres isn't. Also, I would never have allowed those women to host a political event for me. Ayres threw a party for Obama. They were cronies."

"They were involved in educational programs in Chicago. And, as you probably know, Linda Sue Evans told a Texas newspaper, 'I'm not repentant. That's for sure.'"

"Don't contradict me or I'll bust your balls," the senator said. "I'm on a mission, and the only one who can save the nation from more fanatical Republicanism."

"But you did ultimately concede 'yes, yes, yes' Senator Obama could also beat John McCain."

"I said that to be nice. Fact is, the guy doesn't consistently do well except with blacks and elitist whites. Other traditional Democratic supporters – Jews, blue-collar whites, and Hispanics – who we've got to have to win in November, have much preferred me to Obama."

"Are you implying they'd skedaddle to the Republicans if Obama's the Democratic nominee?"

"I ain't implying it. I'm saying it – a guy many Americans think might be Muslim or a sympathizer is going to lose plenty of Jewish voters and their supporters; a guy who wants driver's licenses for illegal immigrants will turn off many blue-collar voters; and, in general, he'll lose support because he usually doesn't wear the American flag on his lapel."

"His support for driver's licenses for illegal immigrants will certainly help him with Hispanic voters."

"McCain's much stronger than most Republicans with Hispanic voters. I'd get a lot more of their votes than Obama."

"Not if he's the nominee. The Bush-Clinton dynasties have already lasted almost twenty years. The American people don't want to push that to twenty-eight."

"A few more nights like tonight and that'll change. Now beat it."

Jeremiah Wright Steps Forward

Many of you who watched Bill Moyers interview me on PBS, and did some independent reading, have doubtless deleted (or at least modified) the incessant sound bites and snippets hurled by the nation's most reactionary politicians and radio talk show hosts. Those unpatriotic babblers – patriots are bold enough to criticize their country's leaders when they behave as criminals – are haranguing me for truthful and dynamically delivered statements about current and historical atrocities committed in the name of the United States.

Before elaborating some of my key positions, let's feed a few facts to the reactionaries: Inspired by John F. Kennedy in 1961, I relinquished my student deferment after two years college and did something for my country: I joined the Marine Corps. Are you listening, Dick Cheney? In two years I transferred to the Navy, studied at the Corpsman School and graduated as Valedictorian. How does that compare to your service record, George W. Bush? Later I trained to be a cardiopulmonary technician, graduated as salutatorian, and was awarded with operation room duty during the removal of Lyndon Johnson's gall bladder, and received three White House letters of commendation. What were two of the nation's loudest whiners, Rush Limbaugh and Sean Hannity, doing for their country as young men?

After six years of full-time military service, I returned to college and earned a bachelor's degree from Howard University in 1968 and a master's in English the following year. Then I moved to Chicago and secured a master's degree from the University of Chicago Divinity School. Like my father in Philadelphia, I was going to be a preacher. My mother had become the first black teacher and administrator at her high school. In 1972 I took over as pastor at forlorn Trinity United Church of Christ, which had but eighty-seven members on the roll and fewer in the pews.

Fueled by theology, common sense, politics, and music relevant to African Americans, I delivered sermons to an expanding audience. I also became a community activist and helped establish day care centers, soup kitchens, counseling centers, and senior citizens programs. Black kids needed to see positive action from learned men. "You can't be what you haven't seen," I said in a 1987 PBS interview. During this period Barack Obama approached me about community concerns as well as spiritual matters. Thus began the association that his opponents now use to batter him.

My friend Barack responded eloquently in "A More Perfect Union" speech but also had to be a politician and stated, "We've heard my former pastor...use incendiary language to express views that have the potential not only to widen the racial divide, but views that denigrate both the greatness and the goodness of our nation; that rightly offend white and black alike...The remarks that have caused this recent firestorm weren't simply controversial. They weren't simply a religious leader's effort to speak out against perceived injustice. Instead, they expressed a profoundly distorted view of this country – a view that sees white racism as endemic, and that elevates what is wrong with America above all that we know is right with America."

That is not the essence of what I have said in sermons. What I've declared, with candor few preachers offer, is this: "We have no right to take a life," whether it's a gang-banger or a president lying and misleading the nation into an unjust war of aggression. I also denounced centuries of genocide against the Native Americans, the outrage of slavery and its aftermath, the internment of Japanese Americans during World War II, the atomic destruction of Hiroshima and Nagasaki, and attacks against Panama and the Palestinians as well as in Iraq. After 9/11 I said stuff we've done overseas has been brought back to our yard. The chickens come back to roost. "God damn America for killing innocent people."

If I'd lived in Rwanda or England or anywhere else I would've been saying God damn that country for killing innocent people. I have an orator's understanding that angry stories about crime and destruction are more compelling than soothing updates on the latest social programs. I do understand what's right in America and have spent my adult life helping people. But that doesn't make an explosive sound bite. As a preacher in free America I'm entitled to some fire and brimstone. Few would've strongly objected unless one of my several thousand super-church parishioners had been a black man with a fair chance to become president.

Obama Calls Jeremiah Wright

(The National Security Agency recorded this telephone conversation late last night and released it to those who promised to post the complete transcript.)

Barack Obama – Good evening, Reverend Wright.

Jeremiah Wright – Who's calling?

BO – This is Barack.

JW – Barack who?

BO – Obama.

JW – My former parishioner.

BO – It feels very current, matter of fact.

JW – Is that a problem?

BO – With the Indiana and North Carolina primaries next Tuesday, and Hillary Clinton building momentum, it is indeed a problem.

JW – I can't solve all the problems of my followers past and present.

BO – No, but you could cease your relentless speechmaking during this critical period.

JW – I'm defending the black church against the scurrilous attacks of racists.

BO – More than anything you've been defending Jeremiah Wright, and very much at my expense, especially with low-income whites I've got to have. After 20 years of spiritual association and friendship, I'd hoped you'd respect political necessity.

JW – I'm not a politician. I'm seeking Jesus, not the presidency.

BO – You seem to be chasing publicity.

JW – And you're not?

BO – A presidential candidate must be visible to everyone.

JW – And so must a pastor.

BO – I find your recent rhetoric outrageous and destructive, particularly the ridiculous charge the U.S. government was involved in spreading AIDS in the black community.

JW – Barack, after 20 years, I don't believe you're unfamiliar with either my rhetoric or my outlook.

BO – Your behavior's threatening to hand the nomination to

Hillary Clinton. Is that your objective?

JW – Politics don't motivate my pronouncements.

BO – Nonsense – you've been a politician in the pulpit your entire career.

JW – I answer to God. You respond to polls and what you think voters want at a given moment.

BO – It saddens me that a man I'd trusted could so impugn my integrity.

JW – Put aside your European left-brain logic and use the better half, your African right-brain creativity. Haven't you intuited you're going to edge Hillary? And now that the nation knows me, you're being penalized today rather than in November against John McCain. Consider that a campaign boost.

BO – Since you're willfully undermining my efforts to bring the nation together, I consider you persona non grata.

Sean Hannity Mortified

I am a great American, as legions of erudite callers daily tell me on air, and in that righteous capacity I have assumed the critical and exceedingly dangerous task of saving America from Barack Obama. If you listen to my radio show, and to be informed you must, then you are now as alarmed as I that a traitorous Muslim-emulating socialistic racist is now panting at the very doors of the White House. Friends, grieve not, my Bomb Obama campaign has galvanized a once-indolent citizenry, and the man middle-named Hussein will never enter our august royal residence unless as a guest or a waiter.

There are many appalling reasons why Obama must not become our next president. Every one of them obsesses me and daily evokes hours of well-wrought warnings my enemies call whining. Someday even the liberals will call to bless me for my patriotism. That's where I start: Obama is plotting to bare our national throat to those most likely to slit it. Remember, this was a man too myopic and cowardly to support our liberation of the grateful people of Iraq. His first grand presidential blunder, of which he has boasted, would be to talk, without preconditions, to President Mahmoud Ahmadinejad of Iran. What astounding naiveté. While Obama tries to placate this Holocaust-denier with concessions and promises of peace, the fascist Ahmadinejad would accelerate his belligerent nation's nuclear weapons program and not merely attack Israel but sneak suitcase-size weapons of mass destruction to various terrorist organizations. We furthermore know that Obama would also talk to a variety of cave-dwelling criminals, perhaps meeting with Osama bin Laden in the wilds of northwest Pakistan, and because of his Muslim sympathies yield to their logic that all earthly evil is the result of the white man's domination.

How could we believe otherwise? For a generation his pastor, Jeremiah Wright, has been one of the most virulent racists on earth – often having accused our foreign policy architects of bringing death to nonwhites – yet Obama professes not to have noticed. That makes this liberal Democrat a prevaricator as well as a man bereft of judgment. He loves Wight who loves Louis Farrakhan who hates Jews and whites, and received a lifetime achievement award, from Wright, for so doing. This hateful anti-Aryan clique is further radicalized by the prospective First Lady, Michelle Obama, who until recently was assuredly ashamed of her country and probably still is except when microphones are aimed at her. Imagine clandestine White House meetings with a resurrected Wright, who Obama would likely award a cabinet post, and Farrakhan, and Michelle. They'd revile All-American values before jetting around the world, proclaiming the United States an evil and racist empire and squandering our wealth and blabbing our scientific secrets.

I guarantee you, Barack Obama is an opportunistic phony who would rather destroy this great nation than suppress his megalomaniacal ambition. But the American people aren't going to stand for it. I won't let them. I'll ceaselessly remind them that Obama considers them gun-toting yokels. He hates their values. He loathes their white skin. He likely wants to burn their white-church bibles. Why can't we say white church if Obama can say black church? What would you think if former KKK king David Duke had been my pastor for twenty years and I were running for president? Why can't we talk more about Obama's lack of leadership experience? Why can't we all be disgusted he won't wear the American flag on his lapel? Why can't we jail him for denouncing the murder of Iraqi civilians by U.S. soldiers? Why is Barack Obama the Democratic nominee for President of the United States? If he weren't, what would I have to moan about?

John McCain's Astonishing Announcement

You know how proud I am to have persevered as a prisoner of war. Even after the most painful torture and deprivation, I maintained dignity and remained a warrior. I am that today. But even many of history's most intrepid generals surrendered when to resist further would have subjected their comrades to misery without the possibility of victory. Today, therefore, I tell you that a little while ago I telephoned Senator Barack Obama to congratulate him and pledge my support since he will inevitably become the next President of the United States.

I did not consider our relative battle position nearly so hopeless as that of General Custer or our troops at Bataan, but I had been seeing, and am now willing to accept and so state, that my political and psychic connection to George W. Bush, my age, and my prickly nature would have precluded the electoral outcome we sought. In Senator Obama, I forthrightly assessed, like an opponent of pre-exile Muhammad Ali, that I was facing an uncommonly gifted adversary. He oozes charisma while I induce torpor. He bugles the future as I grope the past. In likeability polls he's been stomping me as George W. Bush did John Kerry in 2004, and in fact had done to me in the 2000 primary; it wasn't only dirty politics. Furthermore – and I tell you this confidentially – Obama is three full loads smarter than Bush.

Though for a month I've known I probably wasn't going to win, I until quite recently would've continued the struggle and prayed for meteoric good luck. However, after a series of tectonic policy shifts by Obama, I realize I'm done. I, who in several years plowed from moderate Republican to conservative septuagenarian and secured my nomination by so doing, cringed while Obama sprinted to the right faster than I could've imagined, though his starting point was well to the left of mine.

When was the ultimate moment of capitulation? I am not sure. I was dazed by a devastating flurry of combinations to the face: Obama strapped on a six-gun and voted to overturn the ban on handguns in Washington, D.C., backed the entrepreneurs' delight – the North American Free Trade Agreement, demanded death for child rapists while criticizing the Supreme Court for dissenting, turned and voted to grant immunity to telecommunications firms the government uses to surveil U.S. citizens as well as suspected terrorists, and like a good Republican promised to increase the role of faith-based organizations in dispensing social services. As a master of political flexibility, only Bill Clinton rivals Barack Obama.

Anyone who doubts the election outcome need but consider this: Senator Obama, who had long owned the left, must have already grabbed the center, and even some of the center-right, when Jesse Jackson, petulance soaring as his relevance declines, publicly threatened to "cut off (Obama's) nuts" because on Father's Day he had rebuked absentee fathers for irresponsibility and the devastation they cause. A Democrat craving defeat would've blamed history.

McCain Explains Bimbo Commercial

I'm John McCain and I approved the television advertisement with images of superficial party girls Britney Spears and Paris Hilton flashing onscreen before the startling view of two hundred thousand Berliners massed to listen to my opponent. That rally was politically irrelevant and only proves Barack Obama is the biggest celebrity in the world and craves not the enormous burdens of the presidency, for which he is at any rate unready, but basking in adulation and raising taxes and making us more dependent on foreign oil. I expected Democrats to object to this ad but was surprised a few Republicans also thought it lowdown. Thankfully, most members of my party either approved or suppressed their opinions.

They understand. What else can I do but go negative? I'm an old man and a small man and I'm sun-scorched and out of ideas and daily more bitter that Obama is being treated like a tall and sleek Napoleon. I'm the warrior. I'm the experienced leader who battled our enemies as a prisoner of war in Vietnam when Obama was nearby in Muslim Indonesia, studying heaven knows what in elementary school. I was a congressman by the time Obama was old enough to drink, and before and after that he surely took drugs. I'd already been a senator two years when my callow opponent entered law school. I've decisively won all my senatorial elections. As recently as 2000, Obama was bombed by a two to one margin in his attempt to become a congressman. He wouldn't have become a senator in 2004 unless more qualified candidates had decided not to run. I tell you this guy's lucky as a sleepwalker and no more dependable.

During his disgustingly over-publicized foreign fandango, Barack Obama tried to undermine his commander in chief and our troops by nuzzling with Iraqi Prime Minister al-Maliki and agreeing that a timetable for U.S. withdrawal roughly two years from now would be appropriate. And my opponent still won't admit The Surge of troops in Iraq was responsible for reducing violence and at least making it conceivable some distant day we will withdraw. Always slippery, Obama says the Anbar Awakening, when Sunnis before The Surge began fighting jihadists, was equally responsible. Then he tries force me to admit I was wrong, yelping I all along supported the war. Yes, I did. And I'm proud of it and the burgeoning Iraqi democracy our blood and money have built.

Our nation will have plenty of money if it avoids the socialist policies of tax and spend Obama. Never mind the current administration has spent more money and incurred the largest debt in history. Obama would be an even greater disaster, taxing the middle class into insolvency and disabling capital formation attempts by the wealthy to build business and create jobs. And his energy policies would inevitably create more gridlock. As the nation lost wealth and jobs, gas prices would skyrocket because he won't immediately start drilling for it off our coasts. He claims we wouldn't get a drop of oil for about a decade and, in today's terms, that would only reduce a gallon of gas by several cents. Socialists simply don't understand either geology or economics, and I think Obamaism is already deluding guys like senile oilman T. Boone Pickens and steroid-gobbling muscleman Arnold Schwarzenegger, who have publicly agreed with him.

I wasn't going to mention it today. I really don't have to. Redneck radio is doing most of the groin punching for me. But I'll say it. Barack Obama keeps playing the race card. He turned the first near-black president, Bill Clinton, into a racist, and he's trying to transform me and everyone else who disagrees with him into hatemongers. That's preposterous. I'm delighted Barack Obama is black. If a man like him were white, I wouldn't have even a theoretical chance.

CHAPTER 3

McCain Picks Sarah Palin

I'm one clever cookie. The day after Barack Obama's gaudy staging of his acceptance speech in a huge football stadium in Denver, I virtually erased him from media existence with the boldest move in political history: I picked Governor Sarah Palin of Alaska as my vice-presidential running mate. At once people stopped talking or even caring about Obama's celebrity and magnetism, and more importantly ceased looking at my record and instead focused on a dynamic hockey mom who in high school played point guard and could probably beat Obama one on one in basketball. She also became a beauty queen and later married an oilfield worker and bore five children including one she knew had Down syndrome. By then she'd begun taking on special interests as a councilwoman and mayor in small-town Alaska, and in 2006 she delivered the knockout of corruption, becoming chief executive of the largest state in the union. And now her presence on the ticket will galvanize evangelicals and women and thus assure in November I'm elected president and she'll be standing next to a man who could hand her the scepter either through an act of God or my 2012 retirement due to the burdens of aging.

Will Barack Obama still dare to call himself the candidate of change and insinuate I'm a reactionary? How can he, after teaming with Senator Joe Biden, a mildewed Washington, D.C. insider who'd already been hobnobbing in the senate fourteen years when I arrived in 1987. Joe Biden used to be my friend but not after he told conventioneers I'd voted with George W. Bush ninety-five percent of the time and nineteen times opposed increases in minimum wages. I'm proud to be associated with President Bush, despite his having allowed minions to lie about me in the 2000 Republican primary. Regarding Biden's minimum wage charge, I understand what Democrats don't and that is the rich need tax breaks, far more than the poor need several bucks an hour, so they can build their businesses and create jobs and prosperity for all.

In their convention speeches Bill and Hillary Clinton also exhibited a Democratic lack of comprehension about what is good for the country. Old Bill thought he'd done fine work in the White

House because the nation enjoyed a budget surplus and peace when he left office, and was indignant we now have unimaginable debt and wars on two fronts. He also complained about declining income, loss of jobs, poverty, and housing foreclosures, and stated that a McCain presidency would be like Bush's and exacerbate the aforementioned difficulties. That is preposterous. Believe me, when the debates start, I'll tell you why I'm not a Bush clone.

But I will do so in a realistic way. Unlike the egomaniacal Obama, who Thursday night promised the impossible: a tax cut that rewards workers and small businesses; to "end our dependence on oil from the Middle East" in ten years; to "tap our natural gas reserves and invest in clean coal technology"; to help re-tool car manufacturers "so that fuel-efficient cars of the future are built right here in America"; to invest billions in "affordable, renewable sources of energy" like wind and solar power; to "invest in early childhood education (and) recruit an army of new teachers, and pay them higher salaries; to lower health care premiums for those who have coverage and obtain it for those who don't. I am not going to make those highfalutin offers.

That's not my way. I'll instead ignore domestic matters as much as I can. I know you'll support me since I'll be a wartime president enforcing democracy in Iraq and chasing Al Qaeda and the Taliban in Afghanistan. Never mind a year ago I claimed we'd succeeded in Afghanistan. Now it's better we haven't. I need many foreign enemies so I can keep lighting fires under you. I'm going to get tough with the Pakistanis about Afghan and other terrorists in their tribal regions. I don't care Pakistan has lost more security forces this year than we have. I'll be pounding the table. Russia will have to listen as I continue the aggressive policy of surrounding it with hostile NATO nations. I'll also increase our bases around China. If possible, I'll provoke North Korea. And I'll surely take hostile action against Iran. You won't have time to worry you lost your house and can't pay for gas to drive to a job you no longer have. You'll be waving the flag and shouting my name.

Obama Embraces Palin

(An agitated and still unnamed aide to Senator Barack Obama was arrested by FBI agents this afternoon and charged with forging a speech by the Democratic Presidential nominee and briefly posting it on the candidate's website. Shortly before his arrest the aide had also email blasted the following text.)

"My fellow Americans, I must today rush before you with the staggering but delightful news I have jettisoned Joe Biden from my presidential ticket and more than replaced him with the vibrant maverick Governor Sarah Palin of Alaska. Venerable Joe responded bitterly, repeating his charge from the primary campaign that I was unready to be president. I countered he'd always been unelectable and could no longer serve me in even a supplementary capacity since youthful Sarah Palin, in her Republican vice presidential acceptance speech, had galvanized the once-moribund campaign of John McCain. Thankfully, Sarah this morning concluded she needed to ditch the doddering McCain, who had already jealously begun trying to suppress her remarkable political potential and prevent her from assuming the top spot on the ticket. McCain, long reviled because of his volcanic manner, was predictably ungracious and tried to prevent Sarah's advancement. She liberated herself with the frank statement she would campaign for Obama even if chained to the dreary McCain. A few hours ago, he capitulated, and as I write this Sarah stands at my side.

"Already, I have been inundated by the quintessential question: what prompted me to start thinking about this change? As a seminal candidate who has vowed to be different and tell the truth, I shall. The answer is elementary. Several days ago, researching Sarah Palin on the internet, I was electrified by a color photo of the governor in a star-spangled blue and white bikini bottom and a red and white striped top. Standing with legs tastefully apart and her mouth passionately agape, she fingers the trigger of a big rifle with a telescope and looks equally prepared to frolic or fire. That's the kind of woman we must have next to, and potentially as, the commander in chief. I was also most impressed by the skinny poolside stud, in the background, who sucks a cigarette in one hand while squeezing a beer can in the other. These people are bold, they're leaders, and, like me, they're box office. Together, our team will be invincible.

"This is neither fantasy nor hubris. No, this is a preternaturally sound political assessment. Look at the range of issues that, as a team, we have hermetically embraced. Let's start with life. I am pro choice; Sarah is against abortions even when a woman is impregnated during rape. I don't use guns; she not merely loves them but spends state funds to increase aerial hunting during which intrepid warriors, armed with shotguns, fire from open doors of piloted planes at wolves sprinting through the snow. The hunters often miss but the pilot keeps chasing until the beasts collapse from exhaustion. Sometimes, wolves are merely wounded and writhe for hours in the snow. I have frankly told Sarah the latter is unacceptable, and we have agreed hunters must in such cases exit planes, with or without parachutes, and administer the coup de grace with ungloved bare knuckles. Sarah and I shall do precisely that during the first snow.

"Together, Sarah Palin and I dominate the spectrum of environmental issues. I fear global warming will melt the ice cap over the North Pole and flood Wasilla, Alaska, Sarah's hometown and one she ruled as an earmark-seeking mayor; she believes global warming is an invention of godless liberals. I want to protect the earth from unbridled oil drilling; she demands we 'Drill, Baby, Drill.'

"In diplomacy my already stunning popularity and prestige abroad is founded on the perception I will listen and discuss; Sarah Palin will berate and threaten. I excelled at two of the finest universities in the land – Columbia and Harvard; she passed through Podunk at the University of Idaho.

"In rare instances, we augment each other with our commonality. I long ago experimented with drugs; she smoked pot and her husband was arrested for drunk driving. We've both raised big money, I primarily with small donations through the internet, and she from the coffers of grateful oil companies.

"I am, most fundamentally, a modest man. My rhetoric may be sublime but my feet are planted in the rancid Kansas soil of my white maternal grandparents. Like a vigilant farmer forced to watch as his crops wilt, I accepted that Sarah Palin had capitalized on the absence of Hillary Clinton, who would have ensured Democratic victory regardless of whom McCain selected. I conceded, despite my enormous appeal – even McCain called me dreamy – that in order to win I'd have to compromise not merely my principles but my personal preferences. If Senator John F. Kennedy in 1960 could tolerate his contemptuous rival, Lyndon Baines Johnson, who had strong-armed senatorial life throughout the 1950's, then I could embrace Sarah Palin, even after I discovered that bikini body online belonged to another lady. I am nevertheless confident that contemporary Sarah is more comely than LBJ ever was."

Voice in Hillary's Head

I can't help there's a voice in my head. In my place, you'd be hearing things, too. Don't bother saying you wouldn't. Spend a generation trying to be president, you want to win. That doesn't mean I'm entirely comfortable with what I'm hearing. I just can't stop it. Sometimes I really do want to. I get tired of ambivalence.

Right now I'm being a good comrade and traveling some to speak in behalf of Barack Obama for president. He represents more potential change than John McCain and Sarah Palin. But I'm not going to exhaust myself. I finished the Democratic presidential primary with a surge, the voices persist, and an intimidated Obama rejected me as his vice president and selected Joe Biden, a guy who got one percent of the vote in Iowa.

I would've been much better equipped than Obama to beat John McCain in November, but I'm not angry. I'm saying appropriate things: George W. Bush and the Republicans have for eight years been foreign and domestic disasters while McCain has fanatically transformed himself into a Bush clone. Yet, McCain proclaims he's the candidate of change. That's ridiculous but good enough to fool lots of voters. Obama's been telling them McCain thinks they're dumb. Many are rather limited, but McCain's not going to say so, and neither am I.

I'm a patient woman. Marriage to Bill Clinton made me that. Maybe, the voice concludes, despite all their deceit and ineptitude, the Republicans will win again this year. If they do, they won't win in 2012 when the nation's neck deep in manure. Not even yokels will tolerate that. They'll demand real change. And I'll be riding that wave.

Sarah Palin Live and Unscripted

Don't tell me John McCain and the Republicans think I'm so unsteady they'll keep me hidden or attached to McCain's hip till election day. I've already made my national interview debut, with Charles Gibson of ABC News, and proved myself a political prodigy with nice teeth and cheekbones and slender feminine hands and plenty of charm. I'm ready to lead the free world. Go ahead. Ask me anything.

Question – Are you obsessed with secrecy? Why didn't you tell your four children until the seventh month of your recent pregnancy?

Answer – The latter is a family matter; don't go there again. Regarding my style of governance in Alaska, I demand loyalty and confidentiality, as do all responsible public figures. I hire people I can trust, many of them classmates from elementary and high school as well as newer friends from my church. We are very open reformers who've tried to rid our state of old and corrupt insiders. The people of Alaska love me – eighty percent approve – and ignore charges it was inappropriate, during my first year and a half as governor, to spend more than three hundred nights at my home in Wasilla. I did that so I wouldn't waste taxpayer dollars and my time traveling several hundred miles to the inconvenient capital of Juneau. Only jealous and untrustworthy lawmakers strutted around wearing "Where's Sarah?" pins and complaining they had to wait for news reports to learn what I was doing.

Q – Why have you fired so many people? Are you vindictive?

A – I'm certainly not vindictive and will punish any state employee who says I am. Naturally, a chief executive has to remove people who are incompetent or traitorous. If Barack Obama had executive experience, he would've fired people, too. Show me a leader who hasn't axed people and I'll show you someone surrounded by deadwood.

Q – As governor, did you remove public safety commissioner Walter Monagen because he refused to fire a state trooper, Mike Wooten, who was your former brother-in-law and an armed drunk threatening to kill your sister and father and who'd tasered her son, albeit at the boy's request?

A – I hadn't realized my husband and I and others in our behalf contacted Monagen a couple dozen times. Many of those contacts were certainly appropriate. Nevertheless, I fired Monagen only because he was rebellious regarding the budget. And you should realize I still haven't terminated Wooten, though he knows I'm an armed, lifetime NRA member. The Alaska legislature is currently investigating all this and will report its findings in October, and I'm delighted about that.

Q – Did you mistreat employees of the museum in Wasilla? Did you try to ban books in the library there?

A – When I became mayor of Wasilla in 1996, I had to deal with budget issues. My decision to fire museum director John Cooper was a fiscal move, not a hatchet job related to his promoting progressive ideas in a public institution serving a conservative community. Regarding the library, I never demanded that books be removed from the shelves. Merely responding to many angry constituents who wanted books banned, I asked if some titles could be taken off the shelves. In 1995, as a councilwoman, I'd wanted to get a book removed because it explained homosexuality to children. I wasn't interested in reading that kind of garbage to find out why some found it "inoffensive."

And I was not responsible for, nor do I know anything about, many returned books having pages "marked up or torn out."

Q – Since you're a fiscal conservative, why was there no budget debt in Wasilla when you became mayor and twenty-million when you left office six years later?

A – I already explained that to Charles Gibson, and I guess I'll have to say it a thousand times more: my constituents wanted a multi-purpose sports complex, and I got them one for fifteen million bucks. That facility continues to be an outstanding community asset. I also paved lots of roads and built a park and guided the community through a period of significant growth. That's why we had to increase government expenditures by thirty-three percent and collect thirty-eight percent more taxes.

Q – Have you long stated a desire to become President of the United States?

A – I certainly have. You need someone in this job who knows she can do it.

Q – Is your understanding of policies as weak now as it was in 2006 when you ran for governor?

A – My grasp of what needs to be done has always been strong. I didn't need color-coded index cards at gubernatorial candidate forums to express myself. The cards were merely a prop I used to emphasize I can find the needed solutions.

Q – Did you flip-flop about the "Bridge to Nowhere"?

A – Of course not. In my gubernatorial campaign I did says let's "build the bridge" but as a chief executive who hates pork I cut the project when I discovered the extent of Alaska Senator Ted Stevens' corrupt pursuit of earmarks. True, we're keeping those four hundred forty-two million dollars for other transportation projects, but we're legally entitled to do so.

Q – Are you worried that your vice presidential opponent, Senator Joe Biden, has been in office almost as long as you've been alive?

A – No, I'm gonna kick his ass. Most people are even less interested in policies than I am. They want someone who agrees with them and can inspire them. Biden doesn't understand that and doesn't anyway have the tools. I do. During our debate he'll look as haggard next to me as John McCain will next to Obama. But there's an enormous difference between the old timers: McCain won his nomination; Biden was given his, even after a weak primary performance.

Q – What would be your most important foreign policy responsibilities?

A – I would never blink as I strengthened the Bush Doctrine, which, as I tried to explain, is far broader than merely launching preemptive strikes against those who we think are planning to attack us. I know our war in Iraq is a task from God, and we must not leave until He tells us to. My oldest son, Track, is headed there now. That means I'm walking the walk, unlike George W. Bush and Dick Cheney. They're the old Washington, D.C. Warrior John McCain and I will be the new.

Let's move beyond the Bush Doctrine and talk about the Palin Doctrine. We have a responsibility to at least give the people of the Middle East the option of embracing a Christian God. Their God hasn't worked as well as ours, has He? If Afghans and Pakistanis will behave, even as Muslims, then we may be able to stop killing their civilians. That is certainly my goal.

I do not want to destroy Iran, but I will get very tough if I think the Iranians are close to acquiring nuclear weapons. I could decide to give the Israelis permission to resolve the matter. I think even pacifistic Obama agrees about that.

I also want to warn Russia that an unblinking McCain-Palin administration will be much tougher than the now politically-feeble Bush-Cheney regime. We are all Georgians since the Russians' unprovoked attack of that sovereign nation. We must make Georgia a member of NATO and also add Ukraine and lots of those other countries around there. That way we can attack Russia if it attacks our new NATO allies. That's what NATO's all about.

Q – Should Creationism be taught in schools?

A – I once thought so but determined that position was politically inexpedient, even in Alaska, and have decided what's best in an open educational environment is to present all important points of view. The nation still isn't ready to put Creationism in its daily classroom curriculum, but I think it someday will be.

Q – How long ago did the dinosaurs live?

A – I can't give you the answer of an eyewitness, since I was only born in 1964. But my religious beliefs indicate those big things were running around a few thousand years ago.

Q – What do you think about birth control and abstention?

A – Emphasizing birth control only encourages sexual activity. The federal government must continue to undermine efforts to make contraceptives available to teenagers. Abstention is the righteous and only sure way to prevent teen pregnancies.

Q – Do you want to overturn Roe v. Wade?

A – Yes, as I've said, I certainly do. Then let's leave it up to the states. Maybe all of them will ban abortions, even when women are impregnated during rape or incest. That'll be a heck of a big change.

McCain to Send Substitute to Debate

I'm a deregulator. That's what I do. I deregulate and work to keep government from smothering the entrepreneurial brilliance of our captains of industry. They don't need oversight. They need unfettered access to cash to generate profits that trickle down their legs to you.

Business bores me but I know right now there's some trouble in our financial markets. They're collapsing. I'm not discouraged. I'm invigorated. This is like an air raid warning. I have to rush to the nation's capital. As an old navy pilot I assure you this is an all hands on deck emergency, and duty dictates I postpone my Friday night debate with Barack Obama at the University of Mississippi. Imagine me in front of all those people thinking I'm implicated in this mess with Bush and company. I can't have that. I need to be in the capital, preaching change.

In my place I'm dispatching future Vice President Sarah Palin to use her eloquence and mastery of issues to carve up Obama.

McCain Rebukes Childish Obama

Thankfully, I at last had the opportunity to stand next to Barack Obama, in our first debate, and explain to him and the nation that he just doesn't understand a complex world: he doesn't understand there's a difference between a tactic and a strategy; he doesn't understand that Pakistan is a failed state; he doesn't understand that talking without preconditions to those with whom you disagree, like the leaders of Iran, would legitimize their comments; he doesn't understand that Russia committed a serious aggression against Georgia; he doesn't understand that failure in Iraq would allow Al Qaeda to establish a base there. He's clueless because he lacks experience and habitually makes wrong judgments.

I, by contrast, have had many great experiences. I bombed a small, agrarian nation during a compassionate war in which more bombs were dropped than in all European theaters during World War II. Despite my sacrifices, the Vietnamese jailed and tortured me and called me a terrorist. Several years later I recovered and came home to become a champion deregulator who believes in letting the almighty financial markets regulate themselves, much as traffic would regulate itself without laws or streetlights. I ignored Obama two years ago when the callow senator moaned that subprime lending was creating a mess. Any mess can be cleaned up by tax cuts that allow the most talented to innovate and hire the masses.

Palin Reveals Democratic Treachery

I hope you knew, and I'm sure you did. It's hard to hoodwink the American people. From the start you suspected that wasn't really me doing those awful TV interviews. You know I'm really poised and well-spoken Sarah Palin, most popular governor in these United States. I couldn't have been confused and overwhelmed by basic questions about economic and foreign policy. There's a far more insidious explanation, and I'm sure you'll be shocked but unsurprised.

I devour at least two big moose steaks prior to all critical interviews and speeches, and before my coronation at the Republican convention I'd downed a kilo of this fine bloody fair. The trembling Democrats realized another such tour de force would launch John McCain and me into the White House. Desperate, they paid a million bucks to a disenchanted cook, now being chased across the Bering Strait, and next time he sprinkled deadly hallucinogenic powder onto my moose meat. Tests by independent investigative doctors revealed my rich Alaskan blood was full of mescaline.

That's not an excuse: laboratory results have been posted on my website. Interviews with the doctors are also available online. There is more evidence still. Study the many interviews I've given. Never had I shown any nervousness or doubt. That wasn't me talking to Charles Gibson and Katie Couric. That was a severely altered soul staring into the snarls of a dozen interrogators. Given the difficulties, I responded rather well. But people expect Sarah to be brilliant and scholarly as well as beautiful and charming. I demand no less of myself.

The real, unaltered Sarah has vast experience. I've been to Russia many times and speak the language as if I were Tolstoy, all of whose works I've read in German. Every time in Russia I met privately with Vladimir Putin, and assure you I know how to control him. Never did I return to Alaska straight from Russia. What a trivial notion. I instead always flew into Afghanistan to rebuke the Taliban, hunt for bin Laden, and interface with President Hamid Karzai. After that I'd pilot a single engine plane onto a rocky runway in northern Pakistan. Terrorists there know what'll happen if I'm elected. President Ahmadinejad of Iran is also frightened. Several times I flew from Waziristan to Tehran where I told that goofy little bearded fellow there'll be no nukes on my watch. When in Iran, you gotta go to Iraq where three times I studied maps with commanding General David Petraeus and outlined his next strategic and tactical moves.

I needn't rattle on about foreign affairs. I've had plenty. What I really want you to understand is I'm profoundly knowledgeable about energy. The Democrats misrepresent me as one who seeks to wildly drill dry holes in pristine areas. I have in fact personally developed revolutionary drilling equipment that can easily drive to the earth's very core and in the process retrieve all oil and natural gas, and everything else combustible. And I have not limited myself to traditional energy. My husband Todd and I in January erected on the roof of our lovely lakeside mansion a stunning solar heating system, invented by us, that'll warm any Alaskan winter night. The Palin Institute has also thoroughly harnessed wind, and we will soon independently erect a dozen nuclear plants powered by the kitchen-clean Palin Reactor capable of thawing the Siberian tundra, upon which I so often played hockey against local children, high-sticking them en route to victory.

With absolute modestly I must, additionally, trumpet my unrivalled performance in economics. While other states cut services and flail in debt, I tap my surplus and send thousands of dollars a year to every Alaskan. This surplus is entirely the product of Palin-onmics. What is that? I'm afraid it's far too abstruse for you, but be assured my dynamic budgeting, capital formation, and entrepreneurial techniques will within a decade generate hefty annual bonuses for every human being on this youthful planet.

Yes, with you I am willing to share the bounty that is Sarah Palin. In return I merely ask that you be not bamboozled when next I simper and blabber about issues I long ago mastered. You shall know why that way I speak.

Palin at her Rallies

Forget those television interviews with the mainstream media and don't think too much about my index-card debate with Joe Biden or even my sassy acceptance speech. None of that conveys who I really am. To experience that, you've gotta attend one of my speeches. Lots of folks are calling them rallies. Not like those Nuremberg rallies from the 1930's I've never heard of anyway. I'm talking about my revivals around this great country. Have you seen one on TV or maybe your computer? People are crazy about me. Moment I come out thousands of 'em start screaming Sarah Sarah Sarah, and the electricity's so amazing I have to stand there smiling and clapping two or three minutes before they settle down enough to let me speak. They just love me, and not only because I'm cute and charismatic. They love me because I'm telling them Barack Obama is bad. He's not like us. He doesn't view America like you and I. He thinks we're evil. Did you hear that guy behind me yell treason? Another time someone shouted kill him.

That's what I bring.

Congress Mandates New Leadership Model

WASHINGTON, D.C. – The Congress of the United States seized control of the nation this morning, jailing President George W. Bush and Vice President Dick Cheney as well as the Joint Chiefs of Staff. American citizens, and the detained employees, were encouraged to view this as a bold and critical mandate written in straightforward style utterly unlike mountains of turgid and incomprehensible bills ground out for more than two centuries.

As startling as it is clear, the new law declares: "Henceforth, the President and the Vice President shall be the two candidates, running independently, who receive the most popular votes in a November election, and together they shall serve one six-year term."

There it is, a single profound sentence that at once reduces the likelihood of petty party strife, precludes the need to electioneer while in office, whacks two years off the reign of any potential nincompoop, and buries that decaying and undemocratic institution piously called the Electoral College.

The new heart of the Constitution was spontaneously conceived in bipartisan fashion by legislators huddled in the Capitol last week during the dreary second debate between Barack Obama and John McCain. How could this inspired breakthrough have been authored by politicians who've forever attached themselves to a system that rewards uniformity and greed? They simply could no longer endure themselves. They must also have worried the masses they've looted have been sharpening blades of guillotines sprouting around the nation.

By improving in order to survive, politicians are offering a system that clearly would have helped their predecessors. In 1960, for example, John F. Kennedy and Richard Nixon would have formed a powerhouse team, representing more than eighty percent of the citizenry. True, they would've loathed each other in office, but no more than did Kennedy and Lyndon Johnson. Would there still have been a Bay of Pigs, the assassination of Kennedy, the pretext for and then the escalation of war in Vietnam? The likely answers are yes, no, and yes. But it's possible a Kennedy less politically driven could've resisted dangerous foreign urges and moved strongly for civil rights.

Nixon would have won in 1966 and been more relaxed serving with Hubert Humphrey, instead of larcenous Spiro Agnew, and departed in 1972 without reelection woes and thus spared us the indignity of Watergate. A younger and more lucid Ronald Reagan would've then become a moderate president influenced by his thoughtful sidekick, George McGovern. More recently, Bill Clinton would have beaten George H.W. Bush who would've succeeded Clinton and saved the nation from George W. Bush.

Let us, as we embrace this grand opportunity, be thankful to have destroyed an Electoral College system designed to protect the property and privilege of wealthy white men and perpetuated by the claim it protects small states. They can be assured the old system – that gave all the votes, from behemoths like California, to the candidate with a one-vote plurality – did not benefit them. It inundated them. It was a farce.

The jailed employees will be released in January when Obama and McCain take office. The erstwhile opponents will get along fairly well since, in many fundamental ways, they are similar. Once the inbred sameness of the Democrats and Republicans is widely understood, third and fourth party alternatives will develop and cleanse American politics.

McCain Embarrassed

I swear I wasn't trying to foment hatred and violence. I'm the son and grandson of admirals. As a patriot and a gentleman, I thought my followers would be motivated but respectful. I was certainly justified in trying to worry them about the character and judgment of Barack Obama. He was, and perhaps still is, an associate of former Weather Underground bomber Bill Ayers. I knew low-income and under-educated Republicans would be outraged by that. But how could I have known that at my speeches, and those of Sarah Palin, they'd curse and threaten Obama.

You can't blame me they took things so far. Check your computers. You'll see. I tried to correct them. Senator Obama is a decent man and you don't have to be worried if he's president. And he's not an Arab. He's a decent family man and a citizen of this country.

I want you to understand. When I looked at the people supporting me, I was ashamed.

Joe Six Pack and Hockey Mom

Driven by intense Republican pursuit of votes from Joe Six Packs and Hockey Moms, I resolved to talk to one of each in the conservative stronghold of Bakersfield, a barren and oil-derrick-marred community which also offers some groomed green neighborhoods most Californians never see from Highway 99 as they zoom through the Central Valley, looking straight ahead. In a retirement community of solid tract houses built in the early 1960's, where many front yards bear McCain/Palin signs – and only one pronounces Obama/Biden – I quickly found a talkative couple in their early seventies. They have five grown children, twenty-five grandchildren, and one great grandchild.

George Thomas Clark – There aren't many supporters of Barack Obama around here.

Joe Six Pack – People here are patriots, and they don't trust fancy talkers.

Hockey Mom – Obama scares us.

GTC – Because he's black?

JSP – That doesn't bother us much.

GTC – Really? There aren't many blacks in the Republican party, and for several years there hasn't been even one in Congress. Do you think Obama's an Arab or a Muslim?

JSP – No, but he sympathizes with them. He went to school with them. He didn't want to attack Iraq in 2003.

GTC – That's because Al Qaeda was in Afghanistan.

HM – They're in Iraq now.

GTC – Right. And if we attack Canada tomorrow, Al Qaeda will soon be there, too. Al Qaeda In Iraq has little if any association with Osama bin Laden.

JSP – Osama bin Obama.

GTC – That comment underscores the intellectual bankruptcy of the Republican party.

HM – Sounds like liberal arrogance. We're more comfortable with talk radio.

GTC – Right-wing talk radio is a wasteland of blabber and hatred.

45

Why don't Rush Limbaugh and Sean Hannity have the guts, and decency, to tell the truth: eight years of Republican economic and foreign policies have led us into disasters here and abroad?

JSP – It would've been much worse if Al Gore had been president.

GTC – Very doubtful. Gore was an effective vice president in a successful administration and much better informed than George W. Bush.

JSP – We didn't need another Bill Clinton.

GTC – Too bad we couldn't have had four more years of Clinton. The nation has certainly suffered since Republicans stole the 2000 election in Florida.

HM – You liberals still can't accept you lost. Don't blame the system. If John Kerry had won Ohio in 2004, he'd have won the Electoral College but lost the popular vote by a lot more than Bush did to Gore. Democrats registered as many illegal voters and aliens as they could and it still didn't work.

GTC – Voter fraud – especially preventing eligible voters from voting – is a Republican specialty. So is the smear. Strange, wasn't it, that a distinguished soldier in the Vietnam war – John Kerry – was called a coward and a laggard, was "Swift-boated" in behalf of a loafer – Bush – who avoided service.

JSP – Most soldiers in this country are conservatives. Liberals won't defend the country.

GTC – Liberals understand that defense in the Nuclear Age shouldn't be founded on ground wars in foreign lands no threat to us.

JSP – We either fight 'em over there or we fight 'em here.

GTC – How is that? Would the Vietnamese have invaded Bakersfield? Was Saddam Hussein about to charge into the Central Valley?

HM – Al Qaeda struck in New York City and killed three thousand Americans.

GTC – That's right. And Al Qaeda was in Afghanistan, along with the Taliban, and swift U.S. action was routing them. But that effort couldn't be sustained because of the diversion into Iraq.

JSP – Hindsight. And no matter what any liberal makes of it, Al Qaeda is in Iraq, and if we leave they'll use Iraq as a terrorist staging area.

GTC – The U.S. isn't going to leave Iraq precipitously.

JSP – That's what Obama wants to do.

GTC – He has recommended a sixteen-month phased withdrawal after he takes office in January 2008.

HM – If he takes office.

GTC – Add sixteen months to January 2008 and you get May 2010, a full seven years after the U.S. invaded. Any Iraqi government worth preserving should be independent after receiving so much money and training.

JSP – You want to surrender.

GTC – That's the opposite of what I just said. But it is time for us to start leaving. Afghanistan probably can't be saved from the Taliban even if we redeploy troops from Iraq.

JSP – More defeatism.

GTC – That's from a U.S. intelligence report.

JSP – McCain said Obama's telegraphing his punches by announcing he'd attack Pakistan.

GTC – The Bush administration is already doing that, and killing quite a few civilians.

HM – We're gonna kill a lot more.

GTC – Why do you think the United States, alone in the world, has some sort of divine right to bomb civilians wherever it wants? When others bomb us, we call it terrorism.

JSP – We have both the right and the obligation to bomb civilians in order to protect freedom here.

GTC – That's arrogant and the key reason we're in such trouble overseas.

JSP – John McCain knows how to win wars.

GTC – He knows how to behave bravely in prison during a losing war.

JSP – A war we would've won if liberal protestors hadn't betrayed the troops.

GTC – Won what? The right to police a devastated and angry populace? The protesters stopped a war that killed fifty-seven thousand Americans and two million Southeast Asians. How many should we have killed in their civil war?

JSP – However many necessary.

GTC – Is Sarah Palin ready today to be president?

HM – A lot more ready than Obama, and a lot closer to our Christian God.

GTC – Obama worships a Christian God and is a bright guy who understands the issues. He's ready. Joe Biden's ready. And so is John McCain. But Palin's dangerously uninformed.

HM – She defends the unborn, unlike Democratic baby killers.

GTC – Women having a choice is the law.

HM – Sarah's gonna get rid of that.

JSP – She's also an energy expert and understands regular people. She won't raise our taxes. Obama says he won't, but I know he will. That's why we're gonna make sure big-spending Democrats don't take over.

GTC – Why can't you acknowledge that Bill Clinton left a budget surplus in 2000, and George W. Bush, by slashing taxes and increasing expenses, created the largest deficit in history? Republicans are the big spenders. Look at the current bailout of financial institutions.

HM – You can't blame everything on Bush.

GTC – True… Democrats backed him going into Iraq. And stock markets around the world are going in the tank. There must be a lot of fools out there.

Colin Powell Endorses Obama

I was a general and served as Chairman of the Joint Chiefs of Staff, my country's highest ranking military officer. During the Gulf War in 1991 I was the man most trusted by Americans and indeed people from many nations around the world. They responded to my integrity and strength. I'm not bragging, just remembering the man some of you felt got lost when, as Secretary of State in the administration of President George W. Bush, I gave a not entirely frank – some say disingenuous – presentation to the United Nations to establish a pretext to invade Iraq in 2003. I don't want that as my legacy. Even though I'm still claiming we were right to attack, I know people cringe remembering how I pretended some scratchy cell-phone recording, that actually meant nothing, was proof of wicked Iraqi plans. Privately, I tell you I'm embarrassed by that, and I know history will rebuke but not condemn me. I'm precluding that by stepping away. I'm still a Republican, but for President of the United States I am endorsing Barack Obama.

For a long time I have been alarmed by the Republican party's stampede to the right. And I'm repulsed by the campaign John McCain and Sarah Palin have been running. They're trying to tar Barack Obama as a terrorist sympathizer because he served on a couple of educational boards with Bill Ayers, and they're stating and in other ways implying Obama's different than real Americans. He isn't one of us. He isn't a white Republican, that is. Actually, he's a lot like me. When Republican crowds shout they hate Obama and he's a traitor and to kill him, you know what I think. This damn thing is like a lynching.

CHAPTER 4

Rush Limbaugh's Stunning Statement

I know many Americans consider me a bloated blabbermouth who scorches airwaves with bigoted and polarizing statements. That impression was strengthened a few days ago when, responding to Colin Powell's endorsement of Barack Obama, I fired an email declaring I was going to check if Powell had ever backed an inexperienced white liberal. I have decided to forgo that petty effort and instead make a confession: I'm much too attuned to the currents of history to still be unequivocally conservative. I am, most essentially, a front-runner in masquerade. Last year I was bashing John McCain while Colin Powell handed him a maximum donation. Then, as McCain became evermore intolerant and aggressive, I began to embrace him. I did so for my listeners. They are my base, my ego, my fortune. They're my life, and to satisfy them I've insulted Mexicans and blacks and especially liberals with statements from valid to absurd, and I've cared not which.

At this pivotal time in our history, however, even the eternally petulant must be resolved to change. By that I do not propose to risk losing the attention I crave more than any opiate. But I do promise to risk changing my constituency. Ronald Reagan did so as did John Connally and Joe Liebermann, moving left to right in pursuit of ideological nourishment. I, clearly, can go no further right without appearing a jackass in jackboots. Let me therefore hasten to pronounce: I contemplate no such shift.

As I today annotate the considered prose from Colin Powell last week, I fear – no, I delight – that I'm having an epiphany. General Powell impresses me with his concern about the growing stridency of the Republican party and demagogues like me. I too am worried about my tone. In solitary hours harsh whispers and echoes pound me like a boxer hit in the head.

In pain I am open to Powell's assessment that at the onset of financial chaos it was Barack Obama who "displayed a steadiness, an intellectual curiosity, a depth of knowledge." And it was John McCain who seemed "a little unsure as to how to deal with the economic problems…"

Yes, General Powell, our Republican comrades have "become

narrower and narrower" while Obama is "crossing lines – ethnic lines, racial lines, generational lines. He's thinking all villages have values… not just small (red) towns…"

You are also correct, Mr. Secretary, there's nothing bad about being a Muslim in the United States. Why, indeed, can't a Muslim child strive to someday become president? I was particularly moved by your evocation of an American grave. The dead man had won the Purple Heart and Bronze Star and died at age twenty in Iraq and on his tombstone there shone not a Christian cross or the Star of David but a "crescent and a star of the Islamic faith."

That is America, the most prolific melting pot in history. It is all of us. We must emphasize that more often. The man who can best inspire us to do so is Barack Obama. For him I shall vote for president.

McCain's Finest Robocall

I've been hiring people to record robocalls that grind through phone lines to warn voters in battleground states that Barack Obama loves crime, domestic terrorists, and abortions, and that he's a weakling incapable of defending our country and obviously not what we need. You know these charges are true because I, John Sidney McCain, have long promised I will never lie to you. And in that spirit of forthrightness I am proud to present the text of our newest robocall, debuting tomorrow and featuring my own righteous and concerned voice:

"My friends, I apologize if my bombardment of robocalls interrupted your soap operas. In solemn service of my country I had to make sure you understand why Barack Obama is morally and temperamentally unqualified to be president. I also want you to know me better and feel confident about my judgment and stability.

"It does not matter at the Naval Academy I was a lousy student and energetic drinker. Many extraordinary leaders have overcome such tendencies, most recently George W. Bush. Of course I must emphasize that I am not President Bush. I battled him in the 2000 presidential primary, and he bashed me with sleazy robocalls in South Carolina. My current robocalls, many sent by the same company hired by Bush operatives, are entirely different. They are true. And this one is utterly candid.

"Did you know that as a naval pilot I often stalled out planes in midflight? Don't presume my hangovers caused the problems. Maybe it was the planes. Those things aren't commercial airliners. For whatever reason, my plane lost power over Corpus Christi Bay one afternoon during a practice landing, and I passed the hell out and ended up under water before, acute as a warrior, I awoke and struggled to the surface. Painkillers and a nap were all I needed to charge out that night and regale the ladies with my daring do.

"I told them what everyone in the navy understood: my grandfather had been an admiral and World War II hero in the Pacific, and my father was also an admiral moving fast up the chain. No one wanted to mess with me. Free to improvise, I ignored the flight plan one day over Spain and dove within feet of the earth where I sped along like a daredevil until my plane ripped through a power line and blacked out a large area. The Spaniards complained. Some naval officers said take away that brat's wings. That wasn't going to happen. I needed to atone. The only way was to fly combat missions in Vietnam.

"I worked hard, even during off hours. In 1964 I flew from Mississippi to the Army-Navy football game where I relished the festivities. On the way back, coming into Norfolk for refueling, my damn plane stalled again and I bailed at one thousand feet and said fuck as the plane shattered against trees. A soldier always comes back. I'd been promoted to lieutenant commander and wasn't going to let some underling at McCain Field – named for my grandfather – make me wait in a holding pattern: 'Let me land or I'll take my field and go home.'

"I was ready for war. In July 1967, on the prairie-size deck of the aircraft carrier USS Forrestal in the Gulf of Tonkin, I was readying my A-4 aircraft when a friendly-fire missile zoomed across deck and tore into my fuel tanks, igniting an inferno and jarring loose my two one-thousand pound bombs which pounded the deck and forced me to lunge from the plane, swing down the refueling line, roll through the flames, and sprint away from an imminent explosion that killed many comrades who'd passed me running to extinguish the flames. The first explosion caused many others, and one hundred thirty-four died that day and more were injured. I was probably in shock and too rattled to help put out the fire. Instead, I descended to the pilots' recreation room and watched the conflagration on closed-circuit TV. I guarantee most of you would've done about the same.

"By October twenty-fifth I'd indisputably recovered and bombed two Soviet MIGs at an airfield near Hanoi. If this continued, I could still be a hero like Father and Grandfather. The next day we flew toward a Hanoi power station recently reconstructed. We needed to take it out again. As we approached, anti-aircraft fire enveloped us. That didn't faze me. I dived at glory. Then the dreaded alarm warned a surface-to-air missile had locked onto me. I could've rolled out and evaded the SAM. That's what I'd been trained to do, but a hero needs to keep attacking, and I dropped my bombs a flash before the missile knocked off a wing, forcing an ejection that broke both arms and my knee and left me underwater before resurfacing in a Hanoi lake where they captured me and bayoneted my groin and ankle and rammed a rifle butt into my shoulder.

"The next five and a half years were torture, starvation, and hell you all know about. After my sacrifices, I was devastated in 1973 when superiors told me I was unqualified for the National War College. I simply contacted my father's friend, Secretary of the Navy John Warner, and he got me in. In 1974 I was given command of the huge Replacement Air Group in Jacksonville, a position for which I later acknowledged 'I was not qualified.' In 1977 I was promoted to captain and given the position I was most suited for – the Navy's liaison to the Senate. Subsequently, it did not matter I was ignored for promotions or that I crashed my third plane. I knew lots of powerful politicians now, and I'd divorced my first wife and married a rich woman, and was ready to take my military style to politics. I've been a trooper in Congress since 1982 and am poised to be most powerful man on earth."

Obama and Palin Hang in Effigy

Bigots.com is alive with exciting posts. In September Obama was hung in effigy at George Fox University, a Christian school in Oregon, and strung up this month by a critter named Mike Lunsford in his front yard in Ohio. Now Chad Michael Morisette has hung a mannequin, coiffed and red-dressed like Sarah Palin, in front of his residence in West Hollywood. This clever coward, standing before his creation, and next to his adoring partner, said this was an artful display that, while admittedly out of bounds most of the time, was okay now since it was Halloween. Does that mean Morisette thinks it would be fine, during this season of ghouls and witches, to hang homosexuals in effigy?

Obama Dreams of Foreign Policy

I prefer to dream when awake but cannot always control such matters. Last night, as I sought precious rest before the struggle, autonomous messages entered my unconscious and created not nightmares but enhanced visions and insights regarding issues I have talked about publicly, others I've discussed in private, and some that heretofore I've presented only to myself. Today, since you have long been agonizing, I shall reveal my impressions of the precarious yet encouraging future of United States foreign policy and thus the international relations of the world.

Let me begin with frankness not possible before my election and warn that protecting the nation is my responsibility, not yours, and this intensifying concern compels me to say if you want to float among butterflies and flowers, join Dennis Kucinich. To be a real player, and especially the man at the wheel, you have to move right, and I here contend that by so doing I have not arrived at absolute right or even medium so but right in the middle.

That's where I am on Iraq. You know I didn't want to invade. But jump into quicksand we did. During my campaign I pledged, upon becoming commander in chief, to promptly begin withdrawing troops and do so in a responsible and dignified way. I do not back away from that but must rhetorically inquire what would I do if violence increases as U.S. force levels decline? I'm hoping that won't happen. I don't think it will. Actually, I often can't imagine it won't. In that event my soothing rhetoric would be less effective. And I'd be blamed. The right would bang the drum and declare I was squandering victory, albeit victory of a dubious sort. Under such circumstances, you must understand President Obama could not abandon Iraq. This policy improvisation would not be entirely contrary to my platform since I've vowed to preempt genocide wherever it may occur. If murder in the mass appears imminent in Iraq, then we're already there.

But we'll soon be going elsewhere, to Afghanistan. We're already there, too, and have been since late 2001, but with insufficient force. Instead of invading Iraq in the spring of 2003, we should have intensified and sustained our attack into the Afghan cradle of Taliban nihilists and their Al Qaeda parasites. I cannot undo our strategic blunder, though I may need occasionally to refer to the political and military difficulties in maintaining troops in a land that historically has slaughtered invaders. Maybe it will be different for us. If so, better results must spring more from diplomacy than the rifle.

The Russians had no vital need to invade Afghanistan in 1979. They hadn't been struck between the eyes by an assault hatched there. Nevertheless, they invested a hundred thousand troops, billions of rubles, and much of their already-waning political capital. Results of this madness are spread before me in reports on a massive desk. The Russians killed about a million Afghans, maimed three or four million more, and forced five million people – a third of the population – into foreign exile. Another two million fled their homes and wandered shivering and starving inside the country. At the time, half the world's refugees were Afghans.

For their savagery – and it does remind me of America in Vietnam – the Russians suffered fifteen thousand dead and many more crippled or wounded. Bloodshed did not cease with Russian withdrawal in early 1989. Ten million mines they planted continued to be sensitive to children's feet. Farms, power plants, governmental services – the very infrastructure of society – had been shattered and Afghan child mortality flared to highest in the world while the nation plummeted to least developed save four worldwide.

I shudder considering a similar debacle on my resume, even as I vow to attack. Every serious candidate must pledge to attack someone, and all presidents must actually do so. I promise to attack only real enemies. But where are they? We'll doubtless kill them if we can find them. That is difficult in a land of foreboding mountains and deserts. The Russians never controlled much outside cities and some key lines of transportation. That also describes our current predicament and that of hapless President Hamid Karzai. Like the Russians, we are confronted by small groups of guerillas who generally fight where and when it is advantageous to do so. Afghan warriors have for centuries been reviled and respected for ferocity and resilience. The Taliban too are proficient and often don't merely kill, they decapitate. Is any of this explainable? Raised in exile in Pakistan, indoctrinated in madrassas, and often recruited right out of the classroom, many of these young men have never breathed in peace.

So we can neither blame nor physically defeat them, nor can we permit them to again host Al Qaeda and plot to enflame our cities. That leaves negotiation, for eight years the malnourished wing of U.S. foreign policy. You may recently have read I want to communicate with "reconcilable" elements of the Taliban. I pray there are some. There must be. Not everyone wants eternal war, corruption, tribal barbarism, and the burden of producing ninety percent of the world's opium poppies. I'm confident General David Petraeus and Defense Secretary Robert Gates, while outwardly stoic, agree we could be increasing stakes in a bet we may lose. None of us has mentioned it yet, but we know the Russians extricated themselves during two rapid, three-month withdrawals with a three-month respite between. The mujahedeen generally agreed not to shoot at departing troops. I imagine the Taliban would grant us the same consideration.

I didn't say that. And don't quote me. We're going to win, and to do so we need Pakistan's support. That is becoming more problematic as our bombs and missiles kill Pakistani and Afghan civilians, and people in both nations grow angrier. Since I consider myself better at policy formulation than all my advisers, I can't confide I'm unsure how to proceed, especially since on the hustings I warned that terrorists in northwestern Pakistan, where they hide after fleeing Afghanistan, will be targeted and taken out. Recently, wedding parties have also been destroyed. That wasn't my fault. When I'm president, things will somehow change. I'll more deeply analyze the labyrinth and then approach reasonable leaders in tribal Pakistan. I trust some of them understand Western ideals. I hope I understand theirs. If I do, the rest of the Pakistanis and their nuclear-armed military and intelligence service may not become irreconcilable.

Imagine if we were still confronted by violence in Iraq as well as intensifying conflicts in Afghanistan and Pakistan. And then the Iranians tried to push Israel and us and other nations determined to prevent their development of nuclear weapons. I don't think that will happen: the secret I now reveal is Iran needs a stable Iraq more than a nuclear weapon. We may relatively soon be able to deliver the former. We really must. But if we can't, I'll draft Russia to help – the diplomatic equivalent of our World War II alliance. I don't want to pressure anyone, not much, and am disconcerted by U.S. efforts to encircle Russia as in Cold War days of containment. This is a new era, and we're not going to try to bring Ukraine or Georgia into NATO – that would be like Russia signing defense treaties with Canada and Mexico – nor will we place ballistic missile defense installations in Poland or the Czech Republic, acts certain to torment the Russians. One way they'd retaliate is help Iran overcome sanctions and proceed toward nuclear brinksmanship. I believe Iran will appreciate and be moderated by my assurance Iraq must never resume being a strategic threat. And Russia will feel measurably less tense once I loosen the noose around its borders.

Though encouraged by prospects in Iraq and Iran as well as Russia, I'm tormented by Israel and Palestine where there's much enmity in little space. I may have to stride the streets of Gaza and the West Bank, asking what do you want? How can I help? That is also my offer to Israel. How can we dismantle enough settlements, those festering wounds of occupation, and create a map of two states that Jews and Palestinians will accept? To make this work I must, as well, ensure the United States promotes economic development in occupied territories Israel should relinquish when they become prosperous and stable. I was only eighteen in 1979 but vividly recall President Jimmy Carter's negotiations with Egyptian President Anwar Sadat and Prime Minister Menachem Begin of Israel that led to signing the Camp David Accords and withdrawal from the Sinai Peninsula that Israel had occupied since its blitzkrieg victory during the Six Day War in 1969. Many had said Israel could never be safe under such circumstances. In fact, Egypt and Israel have benefitted from three decades of peaceful relations.

What about malnourished but heavily armed North Korea? At the propitious moment, soon after success in some of the endeavors above, I shall state this: Kim Jong-Il, your children are starving, your people repressed, your economy emaciated, and your nation weak and weakening by every measure but military and nuclear technology. If you want to challenge these facts, let peaceful observers travel unimpeded and document what they see. But perhaps I digress, Mr. President.

My essential offer is this: if you forever abandon your drive for nuclear weapons, we will at the same time begin a permanent withdrawal of American troops from South Korea. Our martial absence leaves you no pretext for continued antisocial behavior. Also, sir, those names, South and North, are anachronisms molding still from the Cold War. When the United States departs, and you bury nuclear-strike ambitions, Korea will be reunited.

One must never presume anything, especially regarding international relations, but I confess to being most sanguine close to home. After appropriate, confidential preparations, I will one morning step to the microphone and announce I'm going to the desk, or bedside, of Fidel Castro. If he's able, we can drive to Hemingway's house on a hill outside Havana. From that national museum Fidel and his brother Raul and I will chat only briefly before we agree: a half-century of barking at each other is enough. Having already renounced our illegal occupation of Guantanamo Bay, I'll offer to normalize relations. It won't be much more difficult than that. The most serious absurdities, the Bay of Pigs and Cuban Missile Crisis, are two generations behind us. Let us shake hands in a new century.

President Ahmadinejad Calls Obama

(This transcript yesterday emerged from the transition office of President-elect Barack Obama.)

Mahmoud Ahmadinejad – Thank you for taking my call, sir.

Barack Obama – I trust you aren't a disc jockey emulating the Iranian president.

MA – You have my assurance. Have you studied my letter?

BO – I have, and reject your self-righteous accusation the United States has caused all international agony.

MA – You've made similar comments. And I know your pastor agrees with us.

BO – He's no longer my pastor, and I've repudiated his most offensive remarks. Let me proceed. Early in your letter you preached – a fair characterization – that opportunities are inherently temporary and can either be used to better people or to harm them. You imply I might do the latter, particularly if I don't follow the path you laid out. That's the presumption of one who's frequently reckless and divisive on the international stage.

MA – Now it's you who preaches.

BO – You've correctly noted that my administration is expected to speedily respond to demands by the American people for foundational change in our foreign and domestic policies. My interpretation of that mandate, however, is quite different from yours, as is my view of history. Trust me, your continuing denial of the Holocaust makes you appear un-presidential.

MA – All right, let us suppose it is true. There was a Holocaust in Europe during World War II. How does this then lead to the 1948 foundation of a Jewish state on Arab land? Such a phenomenon is without precedent in all history.

BO – I'm not going to squander energy arguing the merits of why who lives where. Palestinians and Jews in fact inhabit a small but volatile area and must learn to coexist in integrated societies since Arabs will always live in Israel and Jews in Palestine.

MA – How are you going to help bring that about?

BO – This process will be neither seamless nor rapidly completed. But it would be more attainable if Iran stopped supplying Hezbollah and Hamas.

MA – You back your allies, we support ours.

BO – You've called on my administration to overcome the current economic crisis and eradicate poverty and discrimination as well as resolve a daunting list of other problems. We shall try to do so, in ways we believe appropriate. And, for perspective, I ask you to eliminate poverty and discrimination in Iran.

MA – We have no such problems.

BO – You certainly do, and your country also suppresses free speech. Surely, your intelligence reports aren't so biased they ignore the daily tidal wave of self-criticism and commentary available in the United States.

MA – As I emphasized in my letter – in behalf of people across the world – I'm calling on you to replace U.S. policies founded on war, occupation, coercion, deception, and intimidation that have enraged all nations and tainted the image of the American people. We in particular expect you to reverse the unjust practices of the past six decades in the Middle East, and to be especially conscientious in restoring the legitimate rights of the aggrieved nations of Palestine, Iraq, and Afghanistan.

BO – I've already offered my reasonable analysis regarding Palestine. And you doubtless know I'm committed to withdrawing U.S. troops from Iraq.

MA – You'll find an excuse to stay.

BO – There are reasons aplenty to depart, though we won't leave our allies helpless.

MA – You're equivocating.

BO – My statement is unequivocal.

MA – What about Afghanistan? You've made many bellicose statements regarding that tragic land.

BO – We want to help Afghanistan but will not permit terrorists to train and scheme against us there.

MA – So you really don't represent fundamental change.

BO – I do, indeed, and pray Afghanistan and Iran are also ready to relinquish the past.

The Obama Store

I view myself, justifiably and with appropriate humility, as a transformational leader who shall reshape the world into a peaceful, affluent, and environmentally pure place. And I ask simply that you consider me thus rather than an incomparably cool and charismatic cat who on January 20, 2009 will spontaneously wield a magic wand to vaporize economic catastrophes, domestic crises, and wars foreign and atmospheric. I'm just a man, and I need your help. The annual four hundred grand you'll pay me in the White House is not enough. Neither are the trillions in taxes you feed your ravenous and inept government. To rectify matters, I need more cash. Please go to my website and Buy Obama.

Do not consider this a rebuke, but if you haven't already purchased your Obama Art, you blew it. We're sold out. Countless progressive thinkers and collectors swooped in for posters pronouncing POSSIBLE – HOPE – VOTE – SEA TO SHINING SEA – YES WE CAN – PROGRESS – CHANGE. The messages were often accompanied by my face, depicted as that of a joyous and determined leader, and once each by doves and people holding hands. All background designs, donated by professional artists, were creative as my prose, from mystical to realistic.

Click the Shirts icon and enter a new sartorial universe where you can buy OBAMA and KIDS FOR OBAMA and HOPE T-Shirts for $25, Sports Shirts for $40, a chic DARE TO DREAM Ladies Tank Top for $45, elegant $60 T-Shirts, and the piece de résistance, a CHANGE IS GOOD Wrap Shirt for $70.

To enhance your splendor, as you saunter through any community, go to Accessories and get a sterling silver 2008 Hope Charm for $35, a $75 Obama '08 Bracelet, a Be the Change Scarf for only $95, and crown yourself with either an Obama Logo Embroidered Hat for $15 or a snazzy $75 Obama Hat. You'll look even sharper after clicking on the Buttons page where for only a buck you can find almost everyone For Obama – ASIAN AMERICANS PACIFIC ISLANDERS – LATINOS – AFRICAN AMERICANS – REPUBLICANS – CATHOLICS – WOMEN – VETERANS – SPORTSMEN

– (and even those forgotten) FIRST AMERICANS. Finish making yourself a human Christmas tree by clicking other iconic departments in my online store and finding the right $10 Obama Logo Lapel Pin. And don't forget your automobile. Stickers and Car Magnets are only $5 apiece.

Whether you're walking or driving, you'll want to stay cool, and the way to do that is with your Obama Hand Fan for a meager three dollars. Keep yourself hydrated with water sucked from a 12-buck DNC Water Bottle. If you'd like to write me a fan letter, pull out your ocean-blue Obama Notebook, a virtual giveaway at $25. Keep those thoughts safe in an array of Obama Tote Bags for $75.

Why am I still sending you emails asking for donations and purchase of merchandise, after my historic electoral victory in November and within weeks of my inauguration? I've got to be ready in 2012. The mess I'm inheriting can't be cleaned up in one term. Four years hence I shall win again because of your support. Keep coming back to BarackObama.com to buy incredible new products currently in development. By next spring we'll have the dynamic Air Obama Basketball Shoes to launch those wearing the Obama Athletic Support.

2009-2011

CHAPTER 5

Afghan Women Combat Barbaric Laws

We women of increasing activism in Afghanistan do not care that President Hamid Karzai, cringing after a volley of political and media protests from the West, swore there were so many laws he did not know some were barbaric when he recently signed them and therefore will be delighted to alter them to suit those who sustain his rotting regime. What Karzai and other Afghan men fail to perceive is that centuries of subjugation are about to expire.

This is what we are prepared to do. Regarding the proposed law to require Shiite wives to remain prisoners at home unless their husbands grant permission to leave, we will simply walk out when we want. If our husbands try to stop us with insults, we will ignore them. If they strike us, we will reach into our robes and counterstrike with clubs. If they attempt to kill us, we will, from elsewhere in our robes, retrieve revolvers and shoot first.

It logically follows, in regard to the proposal requiring women to sexually submit whenever their husbands demand, that if they grope us we will kick them in the groins. If they assault us, we will retrieve clubs deployed under our beds. If they overpower us, we most reluctantly will castrate them with knives already resting beside the clubs. Some of us will doubtless perish in this war of liberation but with confidence we state our sacrifices will not long be necessary.

Dick Cheney Still on Guard

I admire and respect our new president, Barack Obama, and am therefore willing to step up and explain, in a collegial way, that he's a coward and traitor who will likely pull the United States of America into unspeakable disaster. Before you liberal weaklings and apathetic moderates order me back into retirement, understand that my vital views are founded on supreme insight that empowered me to become the most intrepid vice president in history. As such, I, even more than the putative president, George W. Bush, was architect of the astounding successes of my administration.

Remember early on, in 2001, when I ridiculed the notion of building fuel-efficient cars. That would've been insulting and un-American since our way of life is very special and entirely unresponsive to defeatist thinking. Today, the powerhouse Detroit automakers are doubtless applauding my foresight. And I know you, the American people, are thankful we didn't waste the massive budget surplus we inherited but spent all of it and trillions more to defend the nation against nuclear-armed Iraqis about to destroy us all, and a far smaller sum fighting Al Qaeda which had just slaughtered three thousand souls in New York City.

Indeed, with me as the principal catalyst, we quickly chased away the Taliban and Al Qaeda in Afghanistan, freeing us to go after Saddam Hussein and terrorists all over the Middle East and the world. We were always safer because I ensured suspected enemies receive Enhanced Interrogation some fools call torture. Water boarding and other techniques were essential in thwarting many terroristic plots and saving thousands, and perhaps millions, of lives.

Now it is my duty, as a patriot and draft-deferred warrior, to tell you that Barack Obama is a fool who exudes weakness to our enemies by promising we don't need tough policies. He's also exposing Americans who did get tough with detained terrorists. That's a tragic mistake. Obama simply isn't ready for major league operations and thus naively defangs the War on Terror by treating it as Overseas Contingency Operations, a euphemism for mere law enforcement instead of war. After 9/11 I at once recognized battling terrorists was not a legal issue but a permanent strategic problem, and that we had to not merely deploy our military and intelligence services in traditional ways but unleash them with preemptive strikes, which have kept us safe for almost eight years.

We cannot remain safe unless we continue to occupy liberated Iraq. If we leave early it will validate that we don't have stomach for the necessary fight. It's tragic I'm not still in office and able to continue my shrewd policies in Afghanistan and Pakistan, which are getting more dangerous, but only because I had to focus so many of our resources on Iraqi terrorists.

Sadly, the weak and ideologically pink Obama continues to make America more vulnerable, and every day the probability of attack rises. This trend he exacerbates by parading around the world and apologizing, for our behavior in foreign policy, to many of our most dangerous enemies like Hugo Chavez and Daniel Ortega. Obama justifies his behavior with the claim that being friendly and open will permit us to build long-term friendships with former adversaries. Such a phenomenon is impossible. Thank God I'm here to urge preservation of splendid Cheney-Bush policies.

Ayatollah Ali Khamenei Warns You

I warn you, the iphone reactionaries and academic atheists of Tehran, this is not 1979 and your inflammatory presence in the streets signals not the end of a despotic regime but the enduring strength of Iran's Islamic Revolution which still commands the overwhelming majority that recently mandated a second term for President Mahmoud Ahmadinejad. I shall not pretend our president embodies the necessary stability and moral authority to lead the nation, nor does he have to. I do that, in concert with other clerics. What you, and all citizens, must do is adhere to Islamic doctrine and follow my orders. Get out of the streets. And stay out. If you don't our Revolutionary Guards will keep shooting. Only my restraint, and theirs, has prevented far more bloodshed, which by historical standards has been a relative trickle.

You should also know that although I didn't order the beating and skull fracture of my loudmouth brother, Hadi Khamenei, I did appreciate the burial of his troublesome newspapers. We must control information reaching the Iranian people, and have tried to sever the satanic lies from cyberspace but cannot eliminate everything. The United States and other secular powers want to poison our minds and souls and remake us in their heathenish image. We will not permit this, nor will we seriously consider President Barack Obama's remark that our penchant for blaming enemies has grown tiresome and absurd. With unassailable rectitude I tell you what is absurd: Western criminals oppressing us and then presuming to judge; women not being compelled to live like women; children being perverted by music old and new; my country being denied peaceful use of nuclear power when everyone realizes fossil fuels are finite; the hypocritical outrage of nuclear-armed nations rejecting our assurances that such weapons are incompatible with Islam.

No one should underestimate the perils in our future. Conflict with the United States is unavoidable, unless the Americans change their behavior. War with the Israelis is inevitable because they cannot change and we must. Nor am I naïve about the certainty of future protests in Iran. Though these manifestations may be encouraged from afar, they will be indigenous in character. That is my concern, that our people, having been electronically polluted by sacrilegious Westerners, will in the streets someday march in greater number and in more places, and the noise they generate could equal our roar against the Shah in 1979.

Obama Abandons Occidental

Every time I return to California to harvest donations and votes, my supporters chide me, "What's wrong, didn't you enjoy the gorgeous hills and trees at Occidental College, our elite liberal arts campus nestled next to the cultural haven of Pasadena and but fifteen miles from downtown Los Angeles?"

Always I assure them, "I'm fond of the school and value my experiences there, and I do love the Golden State."

"So why'd you leave?"

"I had the opportunity to go to Columbia University."

"Clearly, you preferred the humidity and frigidity of that crowded and hectic place to our laid back suburban expanses."

"I confess."

"But why?"

"Drive around Occidental. It's as scenic and peaceful as one can imagine. But it's boring. No, I beg your pardon. It isn't boring. It's just that it isn't exciting or challenging. It's not for aggressive people."

"L.A.'s got plenty of aggression."

"Not like New York City," I said. "There I always felt confronted, intellectually, athletically, and, really, for survival. At Occidental, and L.A. in general, you generally know what you're going to get."

"At Oxy, that's true, but not so for much of L.A. In your first book, *Dreams from My Father*, you make it clear, probably unintentionally, that you really didn't get off campus much. It sounds like you made it to a cultural event in Compton, but not much else in two years."

"I think that's what concerned me. I wasn't compelled to become as involved as I was at Columbia."

"But in your book you write more about your political involvement and debut speechmaking at Occidental than of comparable activities at Columbia."

"Nevertheless, at Columbia I was part of a more vital environment."

"Yet, a couple of years after graduating, you got restless again."

"Chicago was calling. That's where I could become most stimulated."

"Let's see, you spent two years at Occidental then two at Columbia and two more in New York before three years as a community organizer in Chicago then three years in law school at Harvard before returning to Chicago to teach and practice law. A few years later, in 1996, you ran for the Illinois State Senate and lived part-time in Springfield prior to running for the U.S. House of Representatives in 2000 and getting hammered, but by 2002 you were already blueprinting a run for the U.S. Senate and in 2004 you gave a bravura keynote address at the Democratic National Convention that propelled you to the most lopsided senatorial victory in Illinois history and then you almost immediately started running for President of the United States."

"I didn't really start doing that until 2006."

"Come on."

"Look, I've got to keep moving."

"If you serve two full terms, you'll only be fifty-five. Then what are you going to do?"

"I'll write and spend a lot of time with my family."

"If they travel all over the world with you."

"I'll be home more than your think."

"And less than you believe."

Hitler Greets Ahmadinejad

Adolf Hitler – Welcome to the Berghof, President Ahmadinejad.

Mahmoud Ahmadinejad – Thank you, Mein Fuehrer.

AH – You've been in the news recently, far more than I.

MA – I'm presently much more active.

AH – Granted, but from 1933-1945 I generated greater fear and respect, and wielded infinitely more power, than the esteemed President of Iran.

MA – I'm sure the Fuehrer understands I don't want either my country or myself to burn as you and yours did.

AH – That's why I've asked you here. We must not forget that a cabal of Jews in America, the Soviet Union, England, France, Poland, and many other countries were responsible for starting and perpetuating the conflagration I so long toiled to prevent.

MA – I certainly trust your historical assessment, Mein Fuehrer. And, since you read the news and watch YouTube, you know how vigorously I'm trying to underscore that Zionists are responsible for essentially all problems in the Middle East.

AH – They're your problem now, just as they were Europe's for centuries, before I implemented the Final Solution.

MA – You're referring to the Holocaust?

AH – If that's what you'd like to call it.

MA – But the Holocaust never happened. It's a propaganda tool used by Zionists to justify atrocities in Palestine and throughout the region.

AH – I know you're a proud academician, President Ahmadinejad, and the host and trumpeter of Holocaust Denial conferences and speeches, but please permit me, as no less a personage than Adolf Hitler, to assure you that I virtually eliminated European Jewry.

MA – I don't believe it. The Jews must be forcing you to say this.

Nobel Peace Prize Conspiracy

It signifies neither paranoia nor ingratitude that, a few days after graciously accepting the 2009 Nobel Peace Prize, I felt as if clobbered by a wet mackerel when I realized reactionary enemies must have conspired to give me this award, this albatross, in order to stifle my initiatives for global peace. I know and acknowledge that I've no more earned this prize on deeds accomplished – as opposed to missions promised – than a baseball player deserves most valuable player in May. Who could've put me in such an embarrassing and tenuous position? Since they've already been blabbering, we know. It was the unrighteous and desperate duo of bombastic Rush Limbaugh and a hidebound Taliban mouthpiece named Qari Yousef Ahmadi.

As the CIA and cooperative foreign intelligence agencies have in recent hours reported to me, this cynical twosome used bribes and guile to enlist prominent Norwegians to cajole and likely intoxicate the eminent Nobel committee of five who unanimously, and in the latter case unintentionally, gave me this raspberry. What do Limbaugh and Ahmadi and their respective tribes want? Foremost, they crave my political destruction. This they hope to achieve in Afghanistan. Limbaugh expects the prize will force me to prove I'm no limp-wristed peacenik and hurl the military's requested forty thousand more troops into the Afghan quagmire. Ahmadi doubtless thinks that as a celebrated man of peace, whom he believes has "the blood of the Afghan people on his hands," I will forgo escalation and soon begin pulling out.

As both courses would be damaging to American strategic interests, I have decided the following: while we won't manifestly increase our number of troops in Afghanistan, we must not precipitously leave since to do so would encourage the Taliban and Al Qaeda, which are tight as newlyweds, to again establish a strategic and ideological aircraft carrier for assaults against the United States.

In my presidential campaign I often boasted, in a chest-beating contest with hawkish Republicans, that I was shrewd and tough enough to fight the right enemy in the right place and therefore planned to reduce forces in Iraq and kick ass in Afghanistan. That's still the plan and why we, and the Afghan people, are already bleeding more. Unlike some in America, however, I understand even with more troops we can't annihilate an enemy increasingly diverse and widespread and always prepared to disappear into arid mountains and ravines.

I believe we must compromise, and so must leaders of the Taliban, or they'll bear an eternal American military presence. Reasonable elements in the Taliban – I presume and pray they exist – surely want something better. To find out what, we must diplomatically engage them at all levels. Thus, at the earliest appropriate time, I propose to meet Mullah Omar in a mutually safe place, which, admittedly, is not at this point easy to identify. Nevertheless, meet we must.

What will I tell Omar and other Taliban leaders, who have no unified command and are likely to quarrel with each other? "Keep Al Qaeda out and we'll help you build a 21st Century country, though I'm afraid you can't be in supreme command."

"Preposterous," Omar will say. "What do you think we're fighting for?"

"For a place on the ballot. Politically and philosophically, we ultimately couldn't deny what you verifiably earn. "

"We'll take by force what we've earned."

"Try that and I'll have a mandate to airmail those forty thousand soldiers."

"Forty thousand more Americans – a hundred thousand total – won't be enough. You had a half million in Viet Nam but couldn't defeat an enemy with vast indigenous support."

"You have neither the indigenous nor external support of the communists in Viet Nam."

"Permit me to sing an American ditty, 'LBJ, LBJ, how many boys did you kill today?'"

"I'm offering you an alternative."

"Your alternative is for us to democratically permit half-naked women to roam our streets and offices."

"We respect your religious and social customs."

"Then why are you so desperate to change us."

"We would never have intervened if not for 9/11."

"There may be more 9/11's."

"Not without increased misery in Afghanistan, if that's where the attacks are orchestrated."

"You don't sound like a man of peace."

"You and other tribal chieftains are positioned to choose peace, if that's what you really want," I'll say.

CHAPTER 6

President Obama Writes to Rich Lowry

(This letter from President Barack Obama to Rich Lowry, editor of the National Review, was posted on the White House website ten minutes ago.)

Dear Mr. Lowry,

I am writing to concede – nay, to emphasize – that you are the most profound and righteous stud of the 21st Century and, likely, in the annals of American endeavor. I have not earned the right to address a man of such eminence, but, as President of the United States, I hope you will at least permit me to beg your forgiveness for, as you so correctly (and poetically) phrase it, my being a "graceless, whiny, tin-eared, (and) classless" non-leader who is beset by "self-pitying arrogance." Please try to empathize, even with one as loathsome as I. You see, I am overwhelmed not merely by your brilliance but that of my inimitable predecessor, President George W. Bush.

I admit feeling like the wimp who tried to replace Babe Ruth. His name has dissolved into history as mine will as well. In a darkened White House closet I tremble in shock and awe of President Bush's (and your) splendid decisions that unleashed the lions of Wall Street on their shareholders, the peons of this nation, and encouraged the former to devour billions of dollars in bonuses even while presiding over companies losing trillions. Only men with brass balls could sanction such behavior. I salute you, and at the same time note that I have been criminally profligate in presuming economic change was needed, and in trying to stimulate it with governmental money. There is of course no such thing. All real money belongs to corporate executives and their gleeful butt-shiners.

You are also quite perceptive in noting that I have resorted to the vilest "calumny" when criticizing the international behavior of President Bush, who, I must tell you privately, is an astonishing fusion of Alexander the Great and Bismarck. In my position, many (lesser people than you) would be overwhelmed by jealousy. I should – and soon will – publicly confess that the invasion of Iraq was a strategic masterstroke that at once demonstrated bold contempt for international law, a prodigious ability to sustain lies regarding evidence of weapons of mass destruction, a "tin-ear" for United Nations weapons inspectors who were indeed finding nothing in Iraq, an obsession to defeat a leader and a nation that were already starving and defeated, an appalling ignorance of the slaughter that would follow, and the insipidity to claim twenty thousand surge troops made all the difference subduing a variety of insurgents in a large and tormented country. I am confident that, if possible, you would joyfully travel back in time and die – like tens of thousands of Iraqi children, women, and other civilians – in order to confirm the critical necessity of U.S. intervention.

And, I will say it – goddamn me for my "pre-emptive excuse making" in lamenting that President Bush diverted our physical, financial and emotional focus from Afghanistan, which shielded certifiable enemies, in order to pursue wild geese. Naturally, I should be grateful that the Taliban has been allowed to build strength and deepen its involvement with Al Qaeda in Pakistan as well as Afghanistan. I could not have precipitated that delightful development. I simply lack the talent of President Bush and you and other stalwarts of the scintillating right.

As I write this, I am tempted to resign my office and return it to its rightful holder. Alas, without constitutional intervention, he can no longer command us. I am therefore bound by the sacred laws of intelligent design to cede my job to a consummately superior man. Thus, with utmost urgency, I offer you, Rich Lowry, the Presidency of the United States.

Once Uppity but Now Chastened,

Barack Obama

Obama's Ultimatum to the Taliban

(Two days ago President Barack Obama sent an ultimatum to leaders of the Taliban in Afghanistan. We obtained this copy from a trustworthy source inside the White House.)

To the Taliban,

Given the decentralized, secretive, and chaotic nature of your leadership, I must address you as a group, and hope that your operatives will dutifully convey this otherwise confidential message to all of you, whomever you may be.

Whenever I think about you, and I do so obsessively, as you've surely surmised, I keep concluding that you must want something. I pray you do not crave the destruction of the United States, and Western countries in general, and the eternal war such desires and your corresponding actions would ensure, so I am simply going to ask: what do you really desire? I know you yearn for an Islamic state to be run in your previously severe and traditional way that enslaved women and, indeed, the souls of everyone including yourselves. In the years after September 11, 2001, we, the bloodied and grieving Americans, could not have granted you that. And we do not want to now. But, frankly, with economic cannibals on the loose at home and the nightmarish prospect of endless conflict in your strange and hardened land, we may be willing to quit preaching and let you do to each other physically and spiritually what we in America are only doing to one another financially. That is, the United States may now be willing to countenance a new Taliban government in Kabul.

Is that all you want? I cannot explicitly promise you that, of course. No American president could. But I can at least arrange for you to battle only other Afghans for political supremacy, and half the citizens of my country would immediately acquiesce, and almost all would soon forget about you – as we did after your war with the Soviet Union – if you simply promise and then prove you will neither conspire with nor tolerate the existence of a functional, and therefore scheming and diabolical, Al Qaeda in Afghanistan.

Trust me, if you do not agree you will never breathe in Kabul again, much less preside there. I know my offer to be reasonable. And I believe you will soon concur. Our intelligence sources say there are only about one hundred Al Qaeda parasites in all of Afghanistan. That paltry number would be encouraging if the whole wretched problem weren't so enormous. In this case I speak not of logistical enormity but psychological. We in the United States inevitably cringe at the notion of your conspiring with Al Qaeda again, and you doubtless recoil at the threat of continued foreign occupation.

Why should this be so? The answer is absolute: it should not. Let us therefore fundamentally alter this unhealthy state of affairs. You quit hosting those few who die to hit us, and we quit hitting you. Time for this sensible solution is expiring. My fellow Americans are accusing me of weakness for long waiting to decide what we will try to do in Afghanistan. No leader, particularly no American leader, can long appear to be timid. You must respond as indicated, or I will either compromise with the military and conservatives by sending about half the forty thousand additional troops they want, or I will maintain current force levels, even if I change the name of their role from counterinsurgency to counterterrorism.

Barack Obama

Obama Stews over Afghanistan

I hope you sensed during the 2008 presidential campaign I didn't want to pound my rhetorical chest but if I hadn't done so and declared we've got to march more decisively into Afghanistan and destroy Al Qaeda, I couldn't have proved I was a patriotic American rather than a pacifist and wouldn't have been elected president. I enjoy living in the White House and want to stay there until January 2017. So now I have to prove I wasn't faking it and send thirty thousand more troops to Afghanistan to bring our deployment to around a hundred thousand which should be sufficient to destroy the final pack of Al Qaeda terrorists in that frightful land. But don't accuse me of thinking we need a thousand to one advantage to destroy Al Qaeda. And don't snicker the coalition will soon total about a hundred sixty thousand troops along with about that many Afghan security forces who smoke lots of hashish and don't shoot straight as we'd like. You well know the Taliban, perhaps twenty thousand strong, is the biggest problem, and we'll have them outmanned about fifteen to one and outgunned big time. I understand the Taliban hasn't and probably won't attempt to project its power into the United States, but if not stopped from regaining political control it would host and nurture a resurgent Al Qaeda in Afghanistan and that would make Al Qaeda even stronger in its real sanctuary in tribal Pakistan.

I don't enjoy thinking about Pakistan but do since I may have to invade there, too. Many of my original backers would call me a warmonger. And so would my own interior echoes, to which I'd shout it's my job to keep America safe and the only way to do that is to intensify fighting in Afghanistan and keep urging and paying the Pakistanis to accelerate their war against the Taliban and Al Qaeda. What good would it be to rid Afghanistan of the Taliban and Al Qaeda if they're healthy in Pakistan, hunting for a nuclear weapon?

And what if the Pakistanis don't want to root out terrorists in their foreboding tribal lands or can't or forbid us to fight over and on their soil. What then? That's a gut grinder I relieve by contemplating the complexities of health care. When I can't take any more health care I try to soothe myself with notions of "mutual interest, mutual respect, and mutual trust" with the Pakistanis. They might be our most important ally the next five or ten years. If our relationship blossoms, and we get our mutual enemies in a vice, then at least no one can accuse me of letting Al Qaeda fester where they'd been. They'll be elsewhere. And there's probably not much we can do about that except pretend it's not so.

Rand Paul Races into Spotlight

I am not a racist. I abhor racism. Believe me, my most painful regret is that I wasn't old enough to march with Martin Luther King. I'd have been very helpful, after a hot day trudging roads lined with scowling social conservatives, in explaining to Martin that though racism is odious, private property is paramount and that he'd just have to wait while I ate in this white-only restaurant. A righteous, gun-wielding restaurateur like 1960's Lester Maddox, en route to the governorship of Georgia, would've been justified in ordering Martin to dine down the road in the colored part of town. If nothing had been open there, no problem: I'd have carried out a doggy bag for the Nobel Peace Prize winner.

I'm a rare contemporary champion of individual liberty and that is why the enlightened voters of Kentucky just crowned me in the Republican senatorial primary. And I'll doubtless win the general election in November because I don't like the idea of telling private owners how to run their businesses. They should do that the way they see fit. I support their right to behave in contemptible ways. That's what the First and Second Amendments are all about. At the same time, though I've been refusing to answer whether it should be legal for restaurants to post "Blacks Not Served Here" signs, I proudly emphasize that I'm not in favor of discrimination in any form and would never belong to a club that excluded blacks or Jews, and that if Groucho Marx were still alive I'd have no problem being in a club with him. When pesky liberal journalists keep asking about the lunch counter scenario, I dodge by complimenting Boston for desegregating public transportation in 1840 and stressing that it took the South another hundred twenty years to do so and that will forever be a stain on our history.

After reading the preceding two paragraphs, you're probably enthused about my political career and anxious to learn more. I've certainly got the bona fides. Congressman Ron Paul, the ultimate Libertarian from Texas, is my father. And like my father I am a physician. Dad was a flight surgeon, and I'm an ophthalmologist who specializes in opening people's eyes with corneal transplants and LASIK. I'm also an unequivocal champion of life and therefore an opponent of all abortions including those resulting from rape or incest. We must overturn Roe v. Wade and let individual states and communities settle these painful moral dilemmas.

As a solemn backer of the dignity of all human life beginning at conception, I am naturally also a profound advocate of rights for gun owners and want to keep the government from entering your house to confiscate firearms. I like powerful guns, and urge you to visit my campaign website and see a neat video of me firing a serious rifle and it kicking my shoulder. I believe there are too many restrictions on guns and not enough concealed weapons permits. We need guns and we need a better defense. I consequently realize this country must have an "electric underground fence with helicopter stations to respond quickly to breaches of the (Mexican) border. Instead of closing military bases at home and renting space in Europe, I am open to the construction of bases to protect our border."

What all this really means is that I'm going to try to keep Mexicans out of the country and blacks out of businesses where they're not wanted and the government out of your life, and I'm going to do that by giving you the necessary firepower.

Obama Battles General McChrystal

I can't decide what to wear. At first I think I better run up to my private quarters in the White House and put on gym shorts over a reinforced jock strap that might weaken kicks from the renegade mixed martial artist, General Stanley McChrystal. No, I decide such attire might be provocative. Still, I have to be ready, and consider wearing loose casual pants and a tank top and tennis shoes. But that too could enrage the general. Ultimately, I resolve to remain in my sleek tailored suit but take off my jacket and tie and roll up my shirt sleeves, opening the top two buttons, and tightly tie the laces of my hard-bottom dress shoes just before McChrystal enters my Oval Office.

You'd have worried too if you just learned your top general in Afghanistan had, from the first meeting, considered you a pansy who was intimidated by him and other military brass. I'd never been overwhelmed. I was just being polite and, granted, a bit deferential among men of the sword whom I was going to order to fight in a hellish land. Listen, I'm tired of conservatives calling me feckless and a candy ass. You know damn well I could kick the ass of any radio reactionary. But maybe General McChrystal can kick mine. I know he thinks he can. But I'm not positive. Maybe I can kick his, as long as he doesn't use his customized nunchucks.

Come on, I remind myself. The general isn't crazy. He's not going to start something in the Oval Office. He's a distinguished warrior who leads special operations to capture and kill terrorists, and so dedicated he only sees his wife thirty days a year, yet he's battered by memos from the former commanding general in Afghanistan, Karl Eikenberry, who's now the ambassador there, and gets haughty emails from special diplomatic advisor Richard Holbrooke and lots of irksome advice from Vice President Joe Biden. And while he feels abandoned by his civilian commanders, many of his troops complain his rules of engagement are too restrictive and put them in unnecessary danger, but when they do kill civilians – and McChrystal admits they've killed many – he gets the heat first and has to apologize to the Afghans.

All that's why he lets a Rolling Stone magazine reporter follow him and his boys, Team America, into bars and secret meetings, and flips people off and refers to, or allows his men to publicly refer to, Biden as Bite Me and says he doesn't "even want to open" another email from Holbrooke and approves when an aide says, "Make sure you don't get any of that on your leg." I understand his rivalry with Ambassador Eikenberry. If I were the top general in Afghanistan, I'd hate to have one of my predecessors write that my counterinsurgency strategy would result in our becoming "more deeply engaged here with no way to extricate ourselves, short of allowing the country to descend again into lawlessness and chaos." I'd also feel "betrayed," but General Obama would've kept his official mouth shut and settled for blistering private walls surrounding Team America. I'd only verbally fire in public if what I really wanted was permanent relief. As commander in chief it is my duty to help a distressed, and perhaps desperate, man. That is why, before General McChrystal can speak, I step up and embrace him and say, "Don't worry. This endless war that's no longer about Al Qaeda and that won't be won is no longer your nightmare. Go home and relax."

CHAPTER 7

President Ahmadinejad Warns
Israel and the U.S.

I smile a lot because I'm relaxed and happy and especially so since last year when the Iranian people offered me an overwhelming mandate to continue ruling our country in the same proud, righteous, and productive way of my first presidential administration. In my unique position as the leader of an ascending nation, it is my duty to explain to the two most egregious nations on earth, Israel and the United States, where they stand and are inevitably headed.

First, I say to the Zionist criminals, in the land I must henceforth refer to as Palestine, that they are doomed. I do not mean their physical demise is inevitable, rather that their pseudo-nation cannot endure. This I shall ensure. I know many of you are aware of the essentials of my analysis but permit me a brief review. There was no Holocaust, and this I have many times asserted while presiding over international conferences that prove the cinematic mountains of allegedly-Jewish corpses in World War II Europe either weren't real or really Jewish. Perhaps they were victims of Jews, who, after all, were the perpetrators of the conflagration.

With typical magnanimity I concede that even if Jews were mass murdered in 1940's Europe, how does it then follow that they should be allowed to kill thousands of Palestinians and forcibly remove hundreds of thousands and occupy their land? Where were these Jews eighty years ago? They were in Europe. Such a sequence is without precedent in history. Trust me. I'm a shrewd historian as well as political philosopher and engineer. I suggest that in Palestine a referendum be held and the people there decide who should lead the government, and those who want to stay can, and those who prefer to return to Europe will be given free passage. Do not distort the issues by trumpeting that most Israeli Jews were born in Israel. They shouldn't have been. This I have decided. And don't accuse me of having failed math since, even including territories occupied since the Six Day War in 1967, the majority in Palestine is still Jewish and would likely vote for Jewish leadership. My worldview still prevails: Israel is doomed.

As for the United States, I tried to welcome then-new President Barack Obama with a friendly letter-lecture about his country's many transgressions and his unique opportunity to change the nation's accursed course and thus preclude catastrophe. Tragically, President Obama still insists on hurtling down the road to failure and has further displeased me with his vile increases of sanctions, which will not hurt us, and threats of attacking Iran. I am not afraid. The United States is weak and irresolute and already losing in two wars and would never be so foolish as to attack what is now, I assure you, a Persian military colossus.

Let me clarify the outrageousness of the American-Zionist position. We in Iran are in the middle of two American armies, in Iraq and Afghanistan, and confronted by a wicked Zionist state armed with a hundred nuclear weapons, and an imperialist United States poised with thousands of deliverable nukes, yet these two criminal actors on the international stage want us to continue to submit to their hegemony and their nuclear monopolies. Imagine how terrified Americans would be if they lacked nuclear weapons and were threatened by armies from a powerful nuclear nation occupying both Canada and Mexico. That in every way is analogous to our situation. Of course, that does not mean Iran is seeking nuclear weapons. We seek only peaceful nuclear energy and, as signatories of the Nuclear Non-Proliferation Treaty, have been quite cooperative in permitting international inspectors to examine our facilities.

There is no legal or rational basis for attacking us. But if we are attacked, whether by the Zionists or their American sponsors, we will hit the Zionists and destroy them with ceaseless barrages of missiles armed only with conventional weapons. You in the West already know we would also unleash Hamas in the West Bank and Gaza and Hezbollah in Lebanon to further transform the Zionist state into an inferno. The United States is too weak and preoccupied to stop this inevitable process. We in Iran have great insight into the American psyche as well as international politics. Indeed, I tell you that our theocracy is comprised of the most knowledgeable and enlightened thinkers in the world. This you should have already perceived.

I recently granted an interview to an American reporter, from

The New Yorker magazine. And I challenged President Obama to grant the same access to an Iranian journalist, who would tie him in rhetorical knots with the information I have presented above. Using these same points, as well as the following, I overwhelmed the American interviewer. He didn't know that friendly Iran had offered to help the United States with its horrific oil spill. He was also unaware we have the strongest democracy in the world, with eighty-five percent of the electorate participating in my presidential victory last year. And he pretended not to understand that the pathetic Green Movement, which challenged my mandate, was comprised of money-stuffed individuals, from decadent northern Tehran, and nothing but a deceitful concoction brewed by Western and Zionist agents. The majority of Iranians rejected these traitors. Reports that the government brutally repressed them are false. Only the most sinister individuals were prosecuted and punished. The protestors still have their newspapers and websites. They can speak out but no one in Iran is interested. Most Iranians are focused on Mahmoud Ahmadinejad.

Obama, Netanyahu, and Abbas to Meet

An Israeli citizen I am but whether Jewish or Arab I shall not say for it is irrelevant to what I must write.

First, congratulations to the respective leaders of the United States, Israel, and the Palestinian Authority – Barack Obama, Benjamin Netanyahu, and Mahmoud Abbas – for surprising us by agreeing to do what they have always been legally, ethically, and pragmatically bound to do, and that is gather to talk about issues that daily trouble not only Israel and Palestine but many other nations near and far.

Let us proceed, then, to put these three leaders and their staffs and interpreters in a quiet room in the White House. We naturally know the most essential concessions each will ask for, and more accurately I really should say demand.

The Palestinians must recognize Israel as a legal nation that will forever exist where it is, inside approximately the borders before the Six Day War in 1967. If the Palestinians fail to do this, negotiations will disintegrate and they'll return to an even more fenced in and hopeless existence.

Israel, as indicated above, must relinquish, with reasonable exceptions, the land that it captured during the Six Day War, and also restrain itself from resuming construction in occupied territories – an annexationist policy – when the September twenty-sixth moratorium on doing so expires. If the Israelis fail to do these things, negotiations will collapse and they'll return to confront more opposition on the West Bank and throughout the Arab world as well as in Iran. If Israel wants to undercut its most radical enemies, thereby increasing its security, which is becoming more tenuous, then it will respond in good faith.

The Palestinians must agree to establish and maintain a demilitarized state that will not threaten Israel's security in a compressed area where military or terroristic strikes, by either side, rapidly put one at the other's throat. If the Palestinians fail to do this, they'll return to an occupied non-nation surrounded by Israelis convinced that what the Palestinians really want is everything.

Both sides must take the chance of trusting each other. If they don't, negotiations will fail and belligerent elements on all sides, including the United States, will be strengthened. Iran could become more demagogic and reckless.

If Obama, Netanyahu, and Abbas fail to make substantive progress, they will in effect have done nothing, and doing nothing is imprudent for those standing on railroad tracks.

John Boehner on the Tee

Cringing at what they know will be a devastating electoral defeat in November, when Republicans take back the country and reestablish freedom, my liberal adversaries are priming propaganda machines to batter me with unholy accusations and images like the photo of my shapely, ultra-tan legs, set off by bright white shorts, as I strike another drive right down the middle. House Minority Leader John Boehner should be a good golfer, they guffaw, he's on the links more than a hundred times a year, about every three days. I'm not counting. The tee-time totals are irrelevant since whenever I stride the links I'm doing the people's business with a variety of powerful and altruistic lobbyists. And let me remind you that socialist President Barack Obama, whose skin is much lighter than mine, hacks around a golf course every week and also plays basketball and wastes hours conditioning his skinny body. He should at least admit he still smokes, a succulent habit I'm proud to publically enjoy.

The Democrats rarely flay me anymore for in 1995 eagerly handing out checks from tobacco companies to my colleagues on the floor of the House of Representatives. That whine weakened after I led the effort to forever prohibit such distributions in our political home. Rather than cash for my influence, I'm given private flights and special golfing vacations and other job-generating opportunities.

I am likewise invulnerable on a personal level since Democratic colleagues privately concede I'm an affable fellow who likes to listen and is seldom strident even during disagreements. These qualities, and my big political profile, have earned a string of crushing victories in my southwest Ohio district where almost seventy percent marked my name in 2008. My good constituents are grateful I voted to end unemployment benefits that drain working people. They also appreciate I tried to extend the retirement age to seventy for those with more than twenty years to work. They know John Boehner is going to keep on working much longer than that as Speaker of the House.

Brain Surgery for Ahmadinejad

My precise surgical adjustments of the brain have moderated the invasive impulses of George W. Bush, who I may next have to treat for agoraphobia, transformed Saddam Hussein into a passionate democrat who perished with an authentic ballot in hand, and enabled Vladimir Putin to accept he could not be dictator for life. My recent assignment, undertaken immediately after Iranian President Mahmoud Admadinejad's speech to the United Nations General Assembly, presented a most formidable challenge: I had to restructure the dapper little fellow's brain in a manner that would enable him, whenever he appears before a massive audience, to stop shoving his toes into a beard-imperiled mouth.

My employers in this endeavor, the most eminent Iranian clerics, emphasized that I was to repair only the turbulent gray areas from which emerge two particularly absurd and dangerous statements. Regarding the first concern, I made the necessary incisions, which may alone have sufficed, and ensured his comprehension by implanting microchips supercharged with thorough cinematic, literary, and oral evidence that the Holocaust in Europe did take place. In an adjacent area, after caressing brain matter with both scalpel and lasers, I inserted a chip enhanced by security films of 9/11 highjackers entering airplanes as well as unassailable testimony, from other conspirators, that no one from the United States "government orchestrated the attack to reverse the declining American economy and its grips on the Middle East in order to also save the Zionist regime."

As instructed, I left unaltered the parts of Ahmadinejad's brain that inspire him to regularly ask painful questions of the most powerful nation in the world. Why did you enslave millions, he demands? How many Native Americans did your country kill? Why have you and your capitalist brethren occupied and "plundered...all the resources, rights, and cultures of colonized nations"? Why have there been incessant wars including two international conflagrations and the Vietnam War and the occupation of Palestine and Afghanistan and Iraq? Why have hundreds of millions of people been "killed, wounded, or displaced"? Why are Palestinians who were evicted from their land, and others who are incarcerated by Israeli walls around their villages, called terrorists for resisting tyranny? Why does the United States insist on maintaining and enhancing its nuclear, biological, and chemical arsenals while demanding that Iran and other nations defer to Israel's regional nuclear monopoly? When are the United States and other nuclear powers going to disarm?

If Ahmadinejad's surgery proves successful, and he stops making his two delusional statements, then the Hippocratic Oath will prevent me, even if asked, from performing any more brain modifications until his questions are answered.

Sarah Palin Shoots Back

Hey, I don't like people saying I'm somehow responsible for the shooting of liberal congresswoman Gabrielle Giffords and a bunch of other Democrats last week in Tucson, Arizona just because last year online I'd put her district and nineteen others in the crosshairs of an electoral rifle. That's blood libel since, first of all, those were surveyor's crosshairs like you see on maps and had nothing to do with guns. Gabrielle Giffords should've understood that and not complained about my map and me at the time. And, obviously, the day I posted the surveyor stuff – don't forget George Washington was a surveyor – I wasn't talking about guns when I tweeted, "Don't retreat, Instead – Reload." I meant aim that little telescope surveyor thing at another piece of political land to be, you know, surveyed. And my enemies are trying to misrepresent my message last November fourth, right after our great Tea Party landslide, when I tweeted, "Remember months ago 'bullseye' icon used 2 target the 20 Obamacare-lovin' incumbent seats? We won 18 out of 20 (90% success rate, T'aint bad.") Obviously, that was just more surveying lingo.

It's just terrible the way liberals have been demonizing me for skeet shooting and moose hunting and halibut fishing and clubbing those flopping rascals before they bruised their meat. And where were liberal do-gooders when some gay guy in Los Angeles hung me in effigy during the 2008 campaign? And another guy compared my political rallies, where I aroused angry patriots who sometimes called Barack Obama a traitor and shouted to kill him, to the Nazi rallies at Nuremberg, wherever that is. I couldn't stop my followers from saying what they felt because I didn't try.

Poor Rush Limbaugh is also being viciously attacked for having a "Straight Shooter" billboard full of bullets holes in Tucson. Rush didn't even know the billboard was there, and when he found out he said, "I thought – honest to God… whoever put the billboard up wanted to make it look like people that didn't like me were shooting at the billboard." Everyone's firing at me and Rush and everyone else who's trying to save the country from a bunch of terrorist-loving socialists.

And, come on, everyone now knows Jared Loughner was psychotic and had been obsessed with Gabby Giffords since 2007, at least a year before anyone outside Alaska knew who I was, and Loughner would've been committed to a mental institution if civil-liberty loons hadn't made it tough for society to lock crackpots away. We've got to start locking up all the crazies. Otherwise they're on the street looking to rob you or worse. And we've got to protect our rights to bear arms so we can protect ourselves from political enemies of the nation. That means keeping our right to bear powerful magazine clips with at least thirty rounds. You aren't safe with less.

Tucson Gun Show

Thank God I live in Arizona where all real American adults can carry concealed weapons without any damn permits, and that I moved to Tucson where we have at least five major gun shows a year. It was beautiful to see several thousand people march onto the fairgrounds Saturday and Sunday, carrying all kinds of pistols and rifles and showing their love for all firearms and ammunition and extended-capacity magazines and our Wild West way of life as well as a hatred of all criminals who give guns a bad name and of liberals who want to restrict guns prior to banning them.

Nobody's going to get mine. I'm packing three today, one strapped to my hip, another on the small of my back, and a derringer in my cowboy boot. If I'd been at that political rally near here last week, I'd have pulled out my biggest gun and blown away Jared Loughner before he got off a second shot and killed six people and wounded many others. I may even have gotten him before he shot Representative Gabrielle Giffords in the head. That's the point. Put enough armed and righteous citizens on the streets, and we'll kill all the criminals. And we're backing legislation that'll push citizen law enforcement much further, right into college classrooms where teachers and students will be packing and ready to blast loonies like Loughner and Cho Seung-Hui, the killer at Virginia Tech.

People should not listen to pink-panties protests that Loughner was disarmed only when he ran out of ammo and he'd have run out sooner if he'd had a smaller magazine. It's foolish to talk about limiting magazines to ten or even nineteen shots. If a killer's going to go crazy, he can do a lot of damage with any magazine. The armed citizens of Arizona obviously need big magazines with thirty-three bullets so we can protect each other. We're sorry about what happened but we're law-abiding people. At the start of the gun show we honored the victims with a minute of silence, and thought about them during the Pledge of Allegiance, and lots of us chipped in a few bucks to help. I'd have donated more but was tapped out since I had to buy a bunch of full-capacity magazines in case liberals somehow get those banned.

CHAPTER 8

Hosni Mubarak Vows to Protect Egypt

I will always be on the side of the poor. That is why I just dismissed my ineffective cabinet, which was not doing enough to alleviate unemployment and poverty and hopelessness. Our precious youth must have opportunities I have long tried to create by privatizing businesses and safeguarding them so they can create jobs for workers, and even radical opponents, who do not really understand what they need and therefore demand rights that are unnecessary and troublesome.

Some have criticized me for jailing as many as thirty thousand political prisoners. Surely, there have not been that many. But today, as our nation endures five straight days of riots and flames and increasing casualties, I feel responsible for the well-being of all Egyptians and am privately rebuking myself for not jailing even more enemies of the state. These violent people are undermining our extraordinary path of reform and respect for the independence of the judiciary and our new steps to improve everyone's standard of living.

As leaders of the United States and Israel and indeed nations throughout the Middle East well understand, I am steadfastly against terrorism. For that reason I recently ordered my military and security technicians to shut down many Egyptian computers and cell phones so they could not be used to inflame the masses, as had happened during the recent regime change in Tunisia. I want those in our streets to go home so they'll be safe. Pursuant to that I have established a curfew. Cairo at night now looks like a ghost town but that is better than a city afire and littered with corpses, which would inevitably accumulate if I had to abandon my restrained peace-keeping use of tear gas and rubber bullets. I have also protected the protestors by bringing in our respected army. The people had been clamoring for the army to fulfill their political aspirations. That is not the purpose of the Egyptian army. It exists to protect the regime. And as head of the regime I have directed the army to protect the people from corrupt police, who'd behaved commendably until the people started rioting and threatening our way of life.

Secretary of State Hillary Clinton had stated what a fine friend and promoter of stability I've been. For political reasons, she and

President Barack Obama are now publicly pretending to rebuke me for recent security measures, and for not doing more about aforementioned societal problems that they, under my circumstances, could not have resolved, either, but they do understand who their key ally is in the Arab World. It is President Hosni Mubarak of Egypt. I'm the leader who in 1991 supported Operation Desert Storm, the removal of Saddam Hussein and his Iraqi henchmen from Kuwait, and for that the United States, various wealthy but frightened Arab states on the Persian Gulf, and Europe erased about twenty billion dollars of Egyptian debt.

Now the U.S. provides more than a billion dollars a year in military aid for Egypt. This is not a gift but just payment for my anti-terrorism and decades of support, begun when I was Anwar Sadat's vice president, for a realistic and lasting peace between Israelis and all Arabs including the Palestinians. I'm also certain that the Americans and Israelis are stewing over what happened after their Iranian ally, the Shah, was replaced by the Ayatollah Khomeini and other fanatics. Who might replace me if violence here somehow escalated? I want everyone to consider what the Middle East, and Israel in particular, would be like if the terroristic Muslim Brotherhood took over our historic land of eighty million souls by the Nile River. In that case, with Israel facing huge and relentless enemies to its west and east, in Iran, the United States would beg me to return. Alas, since I'll be eighty-three years old this spring, even I concede there must soon be a successor. Be assured that my army and the West will defer that day as long as possible.

Muammar Gaddafi on Fire

I'm not drugged. I'm taking medications to soothe my nerves and have for years. But many of our Libyan youths are drugged and now crazed followers of Jihadists and will have to be executed in accordance with Libyan law. My rule must be maintained or Libya will become an Al Qaeda base. I'm a bulwark against terrorism and prepared to cleanse Libya house by house. I call on all good young men to put on green armbands and charge out of their lairs to attack the protesters who're trying to destroy the great Libya I've built more than forty years since leading a coup at age twenty-seven. I haven't squandered billions of dollars of sacred oil wealth. I've used the money to protect us from Yankee and Zionist imperialists. They're the ones fomenting and lying that a third of my people are unemployed. I'm still restrained. Reports that my fighter jets, helicopters, tanks, artillery, and rifles have slaughtered hundreds of Libyans are premature. If I do order force, everything will burn. No one will conquer me. I'm not weak Hosni Mubarak surrendering in Egypt. I'm a fighter and revolutionary from tents and will die as a martyr at the end.

Israel in New Middle East

(This memorandum from a leading Israeli think tank was released late last night.)

Israelis who say we're worried but not afraid are either fools or liars, and I suspect the latter. Of course we're afraid. We're but six million souls surrounded by three hundred million potential enemies. Now the Arabs, clear to everyone not suffering from myopia, have at last inhaled the invigorating winds of democracy and shall be free. They're demanding it. Mubarak's gone from Egypt and the military will soon be controlled by elected civilian leaders. The same dynamic pertains to Tunisia. And Gaddafi will be out of power in Libya within a month. Other nations will join this cascade of liberty, as in 1989 Eastern Europe.

We should applaud this despite our concerns. Granted, Egypt will be less deferential regarding Israel's occupation and persistent building of illegal settlements on the West Bank. It's also true that our Persian nemesis, Iran, with Egyptian permission, has already sent warships through the Suez Canal and into the Mediterranean to hold joint military exercises with Syria, long a provocateur in Lebanon. Certainly, our American sponsors will lose influence in a Middle East where autocratic institutions are being steamrolled by authentic national movements. Hemmed in and confronted by proud and newly independent people, Israelis will have to change or else. That is why we should be in our streets, celebrating more than anyone.

Gaddafi Counterattacks

My opponents are not merely traitorous, they're delusional, and I laughed at reports of their naïveté when told my powerful counterattacking forces had already recaptured the vital oil-production port of Ras Lanuf. "Oh, no, that's just another Gaddafi lie," they drunkenly shouted from Benghazi, our second largest city. By the time they accepted Ras Lanuf was mine again, they were denying my troops and tanks had mowed further east down the coastal highway and retaken Brega, another oil port. I've been teaching ragtag traitors the lunacy of fighting a professional army supported by jet fighters and helicopter gunships. Now they know I'm in Brega and poised next to strike their Benghazi nest only two hundred miles away. Those who drink today are trying to forget I'll soon have crushed them all.

No one can prevent this, and I will punish those who try. A lying cameraman from Al Jazeera was killed yesterday. Al Jazeera had been waging a campaign of deceit against me. It won't work. Neither will the pitiful call by the Arab League for the United Nations to establish a no-fly zone over Libya. I would've recaptured Ras Lanuf and Brega even without airpower. And by the time my bombs have fallen on the big rebel coffin in Benghazi, imperial establishment of a no-fly zone will be irrelevant. I'll be laughing at Barack Obama for saying the "noose is tightening" around me. I'm not Saddam Hussein. The nooses are daily falling around the necks of my enemies. Don't you see?

Gaddafi Vows No Mercy

I feel like Alexander the Great. I feel better. He was weak and died young. I'm the indestructible leader of Libya and more powerful by the minute as my patriotic forces rout contemptible, drug-crazed traitors who've betrayed me. Now, on the precipice of eternal victory, I say to heathens plotting against me in the West: you won't strike Libya, we'll strike you. We'll strike you as we did in Algeria and Vietnam. You want to strike us? Come and give it a try.

Foreign attackers will get no mercy and neither will you rats opposing me in Benghazi. It's over. We're going after you tonight and will strangle you in your closets. If you're not my enemy, don't worry. Come out and surrender, or drop your arms and run away. Maybe I won't chase you.

I promise I won't. I'm offering an immediate ceasefire. Why doesn't the United Nations believe me? They trust those who say I haven't stopped shooting you. I'm only killing you because you're still trying to get me.

Wait. We need an immediate emergency meeting with the UN Security Council to stop military aggression, now in its fourth day, by Western warmongers who claim they're only attacking military targets but in fact are slaughtering Libyan civilians. I must save my sacred countrymen. I'm still ready to fight and die. But let's stop shooting.

Obama's Letter to the Arab League

Dear Leaders of the Arab League,

Respectfully I acknowledge you are key political, economic, and social powerbrokers for twenty-two Arab nations encompassing more than five million square miles in the Middle East and North Africa, and last month I watched as you suspended Libya, and thus its unstable dictator Muammar Gaddafi, from your organization and, at the same time, urged the United Nations – that is the United States and perhaps a few European (NATO) nations – to establish a no-fly zone over Libya and end the slaughter of civilians by Gaddafi's mechanized forces. But, as your passionate efforts resounded over airwaves and through cyberspace, I could not avoid uncomfortably asking myself: why the hell doesn't the Arab League intervene and stop the carnage? Surely that's a reasonable inquiry of a regional organization whose nations comprise some three hundred sixty million people. Immediately to the east of Libya, in fact, lies your largest member, eternal Egypt with eighty million people and a large army recently celebrated for its professionalism and restraint during the people's primarily-peaceful removal of President Hosni Mubarak. Let us emphasize that the most ominous impending bloodbath was in the eastern Libyan city of Benghazi, where rebels and seven hundred thousand citizens would've been delighted to receive protection from their Arab brothers. So why didn't forces from the Egyptian army simply roll to the rescue? Don't claim this would've been logistically impossible. The Egyptians would have met no resistance en route to Benghazi. And, inevitably, I must ask why Saudi Arabia didn't also offer to help. The Saudis have much expensive military equipment and a population of twenty-seven million, four times more than Libya.

I think you know that many in the West are disgusted by oil-glutted sheikhs, like those in Saudi Arabia, crying for us to expend our blood and money in order to fight people in your region who, in some cases, like Gaddafi's forces, you could discipline yourselves. It is certainly ironic that, while Western planes are bombing Libyan anti-aircraft batteries and attacking infantry believed to be killing civilians, dark forces in Saudi Arabia, Yemen, and Bahrain are suppressing the demands for democracy so bravely being issued throughout the Middle East.

And now we learn that the Arab League, until a few days ago outraged by Western reluctance to initiate another war in the region, is complaining: "What is happening in Libya differs from the aim of imposing a no-fly zone, and what we want is the protection of civilians and not the bombardment of more civilians." That is a deceitful comment. You, the righteous leaders of the Arab League, knew that Gadhafi's forces were advancing primarily on the strength of trained infantrymen accompanied by tanks and other military vehicles as well as artillery and rockets. You therefore also understood that Western air forces, in order to save Gaddafi's opponents and citizens in Benghazi, would have to attack advancing forces, and that some civilian casualties would be inevitable.

I imagine many in the Middle East will congratulate you for trying to save Libyans from Gaddafi and, most energetically, for rebuking the Americans and other Western beasts who exceeded their mandate. You have endless legitimate complaints about Western intervention in the Middle East. But right now you're relieved that your best oil customers have again done your job and taken on a local bully.

The ultimate lesson is this: some day your own people are going to take you down. And if they can't quite get it done, they'll know who to ask for help.

Sincerely,

Barack Obama

Diary of Osama bin Laden

Fall 2001 – I'm a marvelous engineer, you know, not merely a shrewd leader of mujahidin and eternal enemy of American infidels. In a scientific capacity I must tell you, as I smile for the video camera, that my plans for 9/11 were precise in regard to selecting trustworthy martyrs and financing and training them. I am amazed, however, since I'd calculated that jets crashing into the Twin Towers in New York City would only destroy the three or four floors impacted and soon, as steel framework melted, the floors above points of impact. What a delight it was – a certain indication of Allah's approval – that both towers collapsed and killed three thousand people.

Fall 2001 – America can't get me alive. I can be eliminated, but not my mission.

December 2001 – Terrorism against America deserves to be praised because our violence is divine and a response to injustice, aimed at forcing America to stop its support for Israelis killing our people.

September 2002 – I do so enjoy being in videos and agree with most ladies that I look dynamic and handsome, and tall as Abraham Lincoln. Today I think about the attacks on New York and the Pentagon in Washington, D.C. and realize I'm one of the great men who've changed the course of history and cleansed the filth of treacherous rulers and their subordinates.

October 2003 – The war against the people of Iraq is evil and we will retaliate and martyr ourselves against not merely the United States but its lackeys England, Spain, Poland, Italy, Japan and Australia.

Spring 2004 – I warned the Europeans. I would've preferred not to order or inspire the coordinated bombings of commuter trains in Madrid that killed almost two hundred and wounded nearly two thousand. I'm a reasonable man and ready to cease operations against all European nations if they promise not to be aggressive toward Muslims. I'm delighted Spain has agreed to soon withdraw its troops from Iraq.

January 2006 – I am isolated in caves and tents and under stars and in the most filthy and modest of homes, and for too long have been unable to speak to you on video tape. Meanwhile, dedicated

112

but lesser men such as Ayman al-Zawahari, the former physician who became my assistant in Afghanistan and Zarqawi, my Al Qaeda leader in Iraq, are now much more active. And why have I not been more involved, you may ask? It's essential I martyr others rather than myself.

Nevertheless, I am at last willing to step into sunlight and offer you a long-term truce. You stop occupying our countries and killing us and we will stop killing you in our homelands and attacking you in America. How could I possibly enforce such a diplomatic decree? Don't tell me that would be like an arsenic-laced Napoleon issuing orders from his island prison. I reject that notion. I'm still the leader of an international coalition against America. That is why I presume to guarantee that if you don't respond, "Your minds will be troubled and your lives embittered... We have nothing to lose. A swimmer in the ocean does not fear the rain. You have occupied our lands, offended our honor and dignity and let our blood and stolen our money and destroyed our houses... and we will give you the same treatment.

"You have tried to prevent us from leading a dignified life, but you will not be able to prevent us from a dignified death. Failing to carry our jihad, which is called for in our religion, is a sin. The best death to us is under the shadows of swords. Don't let your strength and modern arms fool you. They win a few battles but lose the war. Patience and steadfastness are much better. We were patient in fighting the Soviet Union with simple weapons for ten years and we bled their economy and now they are nothing.

"In that there is a lesson for you."

You see why enemy forces hunt me without cease. I can kill with planes or words, and am by bounds the most articulate man in this war. All Bush and Cheney have said is they don't negotiate with terrorists. They only destroy them. So how will this war ever end? You won't negotiate with those you re fighting, and your leaders forever insist – their need for enemies is as unrelenting as mine – that you are indeed in a real war. Of course, if a nation as vast as America really were at war, wouldn't it have ten percent of its population under arms, as during Word War Two? Instead, you struggle, and often fail, to meet even the most modest recruiting requirements. And yet you're talking evermore of also attacking Iran. I hope you will not do so but have always considered your invasion of Iraq a preliminary step to assaulting our Muslim brothers to the east.

At this instant I for the first time foresee that even in abject hiding I can do much more than infrequently deliver tapes of appalling technical quality. I really do understand America. And I know you would never negotiate with me. So if you agree to negotiate with leaders who were not involved in September Eleventh, pursuant to withdrawing from Muslim territories in exchange for our vow not to attack you at home or anywhere else, I will send you my dissipated head on a golden platter.

Spring 2006 – I'm still sacrificing so much and have since leaving a Saudi Arabian family of vast wealth and fighting the Russians in the wilds of Afghanistan and then starting to hit the Americans. After 9/11 I've dwelled in a series of ruts, enduring these travails with stoicism and undiminished resolve, but recently decided to buy a large lot in a peaceful Abbottabad neighborhood near the national military academy and build this custom three-story home surrounded by high walls topped with barbed wire and nestled close to pretty hills that my wives and children and a few intimates can gaze at through small windows but never visit. We have to stay inside the walls, except when we travel at night to other Pakistani places.

May 2006 – I masterminded the 9/11 attacks and am sick of others getting credit and getting convicted.

September 2007 – Six glorious years have passed since last I struck hard enough so today I warn Americans I'll intensify the war in Iraq and they're vulnerable despite economic and military might.

March 2008 – I may strike the Europeans because of their evil cartoons of the Prophet Muhammad. And I urge all Muslims to help their Palestinian brothers by fighting against the odious Iraqi government and the United States.

May 2008 – Western peoples beware: I'm calling for intensified fighting against Israel because the Israeli-Palestinian conflict is at the heart of the Muslim battle with the West. I further urge Muslims to smash Israel's blockade of Gaza and fight all Arab governments that deal with Israel.

March 2009 – Traitorous Arab leaders plotted with the West to undermine Islam and aid Israel in its three-week assault of Gaza.

June 2009 – Barack Obama is black outside and son of a Muslim father but white inside and a Christian heathen who has sown revenge and hatred of America in the Muslim world. Americans must now prepare for the consequences.

September 2009 – Obama can't win the wars in Afghanistan and Iraq nor can he stop the indigenous people from fighting. He better do something he can and control the neo-conservatives and Israeli lobby. Remember, the reason for our dispute with you is your support for Israel occupying our land in Palestine.

April 2011 – Many Arabs are calling me anachronistic and irrelevant. They claim secular and educated young people are leading the democratic revolutions in Tunisia and Egypt and Libya and Bahrain and Yemen. They wouldn't be having so much success without my actions. They should remember that.

May 2011 – Which one of my wives am I in bed with? Suddenly I don't know because helicopters are entering my compound and I jump up as shots erupt outside and then inside my home and I sense my brother and adult son and trusted courier are dead. Boots pound stairs and strange shouts shatter the walls. Room by room they're searching, honing in now on the third floor. I have nowhere to go. I hold no gun. When Americans storm into my bedroom I simply stare as they fire bullets into my head and chest.

The infidels at first try to defame me with the lie I jerked one of my wives in front of me but that claim was too crude to last more than a few hours. She voluntarily charged my enemies and was wounded in the leg. A warrior never hides behind a woman.

I will, however reluctantly, thank Obama for ordering that my body, in traditional Muslim fashion, be bathed and wrapped in a white sheet and placed on a flat board, in that most unlikely location, the deck of an aircraft carrier, prior to being dumped into the Arabian Sea only twelve hours after martyrdom.

Interview with Rick Perry

(Late last night, after being driven to a confidential location, I interviewed Republican presidential candidate Rick Perry.)

George Thomas Clark – Good evening, Governor Perry.

Rick Perry – Howdy.

GTC – You've been touting, rather loudly, your record as a producer of jobs in the state of Texas.

RP – Damn right. Texas, under my leadership, has generated 237,000 new jobs the last two years, more than any other state.

GTC – I was impressed by that until I studied some of the facts. For example, as of this month the national unemployment figure is 9.1% while in Texas it's only modestly lower at 8.4%. Economists say that's the worst in Texas in a quarter of a century.

RP – President Barack Obama is destroying jobs with his socialist policies and government giveaways. He's the problem in Texas and the whole country.

GTC – Shouldn't you thank the president for the stimulus money you've received? In 2010 you and Texas asked the federal government for and were rewarded $6.4 billion "to help balance the budget. Ninety-seven percent of the budget shortfall was filled with stimulus money." You also received another $5.7 billion in aid for "programs such as highway and bridge construction, child care development programs and weatherization assistance." And as of June 2011 Texas had received $17.4 billion in stimulus money, second most in the country.

RP – We wouldn't have needed that money in the first place if the Obama administration hadn't created an environment hostile to businesses and the entrepreneurs who run them. In Texas we're different. We don't have a state income tax, and we don't pile on environmental regulations. We understand job formation.

GTC – What kinds of jobs? The latest figures are that in Texas 9.54% of the workers earn the minimum wage or less. That's the highest rate in the United States. Mississippi is second worst at 9.50%. The national average for those low wages is 6.0%.

RP – Most people have to start low and work their way up. That's how progress is made. I know that because "I'm a full-throated, unapologetic fiscal conservative." And I'm proud to tell you I'm against Obama's socialist universal health care policies. Requiring people to buy health insurance is un-American.

GTC – People who drive are required to purchase auto insurance. This is similar in principle. Aren't you concerned that more than a quarter of Texans – 26% – don't have health insurance? The national average is 17%.

RP – Hey, I've been Governor of Texas longer than anyone in history. You bet I'm concerned. Look at my website. You'll see I've led Texas to the "forefront in innovative efforts to control medical costs, utilizing market-based solutions to improve the quality of treatments and wide access to care for all Texans. (I've) called for a rejection of federal mandates, and instead promoted state-based solutions."

One of my most important accomplishments is reforming the "medical liability tort system in 2003. Before that, out-of-control trial lawyers were suing Texas doctors at twice the national rate, and had forced many doctors into a tough decision: leave Texas or give up medicine altogether... Today, doctors are applying to care for Texans in record numbers."

GTC – Many in Texas will continue to be either medically uninsured or under-insured as long as the state struggles educationally. Texas has the lowest percentage of adults with high school diplomas in the country. The state's also near the bottom in SAT scores. Teacher salaries haven't kept pace with those in states with better academic results.

RP – Our teachers will have higher salaries and smaller classes when I turn this economy around. That'll be done with money generated by the private sector, not the government. Remember, governments don't generate a dime. They only tax and spend.

In my career as a public servant I've "worked to raise the overall quality of education in Texas by aligning the higher education standards more closely with the needs of business, balancing accountability with incentives for teacher and school performance and increasing the emphasis on core subject areas like math, reading and science."

GTC – You oppose virtually all abortions and are therefore an opponent of Roe V. Wade.

RP – That's right. "I'm pro-life," and, I should add, "pro-traditional marriage." In 2005 I signed legislation "giving parents the right to consent before their minor daughters can have an abortion. (It was an) effort to create a culture of life by protecting those who can't protect themselves, by giving voice to the voiceless who yearn for life." That same day I also "signed a constitutional amendment that (defined) marriage as a union between a man and a woman… History tells us, and most Texans believe, that marriage exists for more than the convenience of consenting adults, but also for the eternal benefit of our children."

This May I also signed the "Mandatory Ultrasound Bill" requiring that a sonogram be performed before any abortion "sedative or anesthesia is administered." That way the woman can "see the sonogram images of the unborn child and hear the heartbeat along with a verbal explanation of the heartbeat" before she makes a tragic mistake.

GTC – In 2006 you attended a sermon in San Antonio by the Rev. John Hagee, who declared, "If you live your life and don't confess your sins to God Almighty through the authority of Christ and His blood, I'm going to say this very plainly, you're going straight to hell with a nonstop ticket." Afterward, you were asked if you agreed, and you said, "It's my faith, and I'm a believer." In the United States we have a vital, and once-cherished, separation of church and state. Do you believe in the separation of church and state?

RP – I believe in the separation of church and state but people of faith cannot and must not lose their faith when making political decisions in office.

GTC – You've stated that you're a "firm believer in intelligent design as a matter of faith and intellect." And you want it taught in school along with evolution.

RP – That's right. Evolution is only a theory and not the word of God.

Sarah Palin Gazes at 2012

Listen, some people have been saying I'm jealous of Michele Bachmann since she's been getting all the publicity and won some straw poll in Iowa. That's silly. I could've won that but didn't want to sweat for something nobody cares about. That's why I quit as Governor of Alaska. I was bored as well as sick of spending a half million dollars to defend myself against liars who claimed I had some ethical violations. After having traveled around this great country and thrilled honest citizens during the 2008 presidential campaign, I had to find something exciting and did that by getting my own reality TV show and letting people see I really am as regular with my family as when telling big angry crowds that Barack Obama digs terrorists.

I haven't decided whether I'm running for president or I'd tell you. So far I haven't needed to get down and dirty with those other candidates. They don't have my popularity and charisma. Let them keep knocking each other off. I'm not worried I've been sinking in the polls. Let me tell you, that would change in two seconds if I announced my candidacy. Look how that unknown Texas governor, Rick Perry, has rocketed into the lead. He didn't do anything except excite people, and that's what I do best.

I know I could win the Republican primary and the general election. I just don't know if I want to. I want to be president but don't really want to go through the primaries. And, frankly, I thought the people by now would've spared me the hassle by demanding I run and that the others step aside. Even like it has been, when I'm out mixing and giving speeches, people all tell me I'm the one. I guess I'll have to run. If I don't, the liberals will say Palin quit as governor because she really doesn't want a job, all she wants is to be a celebrity. The former isn't true, but, yeah, I do like being famous and know in order to become really powerful I've got to go ahead and do it. And here's what's going to happen.

Michele Bachmann – She's going to look old next to me and people will start talking about that instead of how pretty she is. And she doesn't move people the way I do. We've got the same righteous base, and most of those folks will immediately get behind me when

I jump into the race. And let's be honest, Bachmann's chubby, high-voiced husband is pretty dorky and becoming a national joke and not at all an asset like my chiseled, dog-sledding Todd.

Rick Perry – Like Bachmann, this guy's got about the same base, very down to earth folks who're pro God, anti science, pro death penalty, anti abortion, pro guns, and not very well educated. I probably own more guns than Rick Perry and have done more hunting and will challenge him on that if he tries to get macho. And if he brags about having been governor of Texas longer than anyone in history, and asks why I quit in Alaska, I'll remind him Alaska's twice as big as Texas and that I'd already done more there than he'll ever do in his state. I've also been doing a lot more homework than in 2008 and am not going to let the liberals again portray me as an airhead. Perry has no national experience, and his gaffes about Texas seceding from the nation and Fed Chief Ben Bernacke being "treasonous" have already hurt him. Now I'm the experienced, careful-speaking national candidate.

Mitt Romney – This guy puts people to sleep. Imagine me on stage head to head with him. The crowd would be chanting, "Sarah, Sarah," and I'd be smiling and just pumping, and ole Mitt would be standing there in starched underwear. Then I'd smack him with reminders that his socialist Obama-care health program, when he was Governor of Massachusetts, is responsible for lots of our problems. Really, I'd be all over Mitt, figuratively speaking, and people would remember why they'd forgotten him.

Ron Paul – We know this little old man isn't going to get the nomination but I wouldn't pancake the poor guy unless he got smart aleck with me. He wants a weak America overseas. I'd poke him with that. Come on. Put the two of us before the voters and you know who'd they'd choose.

Barack Obama – I'm not worried about my weak opposition in the Republican primary. And I'm not worried about Obama, either. John McCain was his greatest ally in 2008, preventing me from fully exploiting Obama, the lover of terrorists. I'm going to hurt the president with that. But the most important thing is the bad job he's done. Look at the economy. We never had problems like that when I was mayor of Wasilla or Governor of Alaska. I've been a businessperson and know what it takes to create jobs, which Obama can't do even giving away trillions of the taxpayers' dollars. The people wanted someone different in 2008, and they got someone very different and strange and not like most of us. People do need change, but they still want someone who's one of them. In this great country, there's only one person like that.

Personal Note – I want you to remember, though, that if my huge family asks me to think of them first and take a job that lets me spend more time with them – probably another reality TV show – then I'll have to do it because for me family is more important than for power-hungry candidates.

CHAPTER 9

Obama's Afghan Nightmare

I wish I could sleep better but feel almost awake hearing August 2011 was the deadliest month for our soldiers in our longest (but not bloodiest) war. It had to become our longest because during the 2008 campaign I proved I was as belligerent as opponents by vowing to escalate military operations in Afghanistan and destroy Al Qaeda. I know there hasn't been much Al Qaeda to destroy there and that bothers me. I deflect my discomfort by vowing to defeat or at least pacify the Taliban despite knowing we can't appreciably damage those implacable warriors who, let us admit, are battling for their homeland. Our current hundred thousand soldiers and much smaller contingent of increasingly reluctant allies are not remotely sufficient and five times that many wouldn't be, either.

No president could state that and be reelected, and I, like all presidents, will say or neglect to say most anything that improves my odds of staying in office. For that reason I'm grinding my teeth and clenching the covers as I toss back and forth in bed unable to forget sixty-six Americans died in Afghanistan last month and that number won't appreciably drop due to my primarily-political withdrawal of ten thousand soldiers this year and twenty-three thousand more by next summer, when I pray I'll be able to claim not merely a diminished U.S. presence but a miraculous rout of the enemy.

On this endless night what I really see are about sixty-eight thousand Americans killing lots of Taliban soldiers, who'll rapidly be replaced, as well as plenty of civilians and losing several hundred more of our soldiers and dealing with corrupt President Hamid Karzai and his henchmen who loathe us but want us there fighting until the end of 2014 when they'll either ask us to keep fighting or, if their troops and security forces, dutifully trained and lavishly financed by the United States, are moderately competent, to stay and continue training and supporting them. And I, or another president, will have to claim that Al Qaeda, which is more numerous in Pakistan and Yemen, and which planned much of 9/11 in Germany, is somehow preordained to again strike us while its new brain trust is bunkered in Afghanistan. That is what I must pretend to believe. That is what most Americans either believe or pretend to believe. And that is why I have vowed to keep fighting until we can bring this war to a "responsible end." That reminds me of Richard Nixon insisting on "peace with honor" in Viet Nam. And that's a nightmare from which I shall awake in a hellish place.

Crimes Against Iraqi Women

When I was twelve my father, a failed shopkeeper, received money and jewelry from an old man of forty who took me as his wife. The first time alone was a nightmare like every time before another old man, who I'm sure paid my husband, took me to live in a large old house surrounded by battered walls with several of "his women," four girls about my age. Three told me they'd been kidnapped, and the other, like me, was a salable wife. The new old man grabbed whichever of us he wanted for the night but soon focused on renting our bodies to men from young to old and dirty who did what they pleased and snickered about the superiority of "young stuff."

We moved to cities and towns around Iraq wherever the old man heard business was good. He always told us to be nice to the men or else he'd slap us. I wanted to kill him and might have but was arrested for prostitution and in jail several months. I didn't want to go home but had nowhere else. When I got there my family called me filth and said get away before I shamed them more. I don't have a real home but found a little better old man who sometimes appreciates the money I earn and may let me learn to read.

Bashar al-Assad Defends Himself

It's unfair many people are calling me a cutthroat. I'm an eye doctor who studied medicine in London and speaks English quite well. My beautiful wife is British, and those who've actually met us often say we're a seductive couple and emphasize I'm a modern man capable of reforming Syria. Indeed, I'm an updated and enlightened version of my father, President Hafez al-Assad, leader of Syria for some thirty years until I assumed command following his death in 2000.

My father had to nullify twenty thousand traitorous Syrians who challenged his rule in 1982. My current counterstrikes in defense of the nation are still by comparison rather modest and have only eliminated about three thousand internal Syrian enemies who were demanding I relinquish my office. I'm continuing to respond with commendable restraint and only arresting and torturing those who deserve it and never cutting off water and electricity and the internet unless those services are being used to threaten law and order, which I personify as president.

Thankfully, I control the military, and have resolved to continue to protect my people, most of whom love me, and remain a farsighted leader and the only one who can properly govern Syria. In that regard, I'm offering to grant modest concessions, even to the increasing numbers who've betrayed the land I love and, in a sense, own.

Free and Happy in Saudi Arabia

I ask you to be nuanced and refrain from mistakenly lumping me with that herd of Wahhabi Muslim clerics who crave keeping women masked and Saudi Arabia manacled in the Middle Ages. Though aged and inbred, I, King Abdullah, have transcended some of the most repressive tendencies of my country, region, and religion, and have as well rather nervously noted the abrupt expulsion of President Ben Ali from Tunisia, the infirmed President Mubarak wheezing on a stretcher inside a glass cage in an Egyptian courtroom, and bombs detonating where Libyan rebels and NATO believed Colonel Gaddafi was hiding. After rebels attacked and severely wounded President Saleh of Yemen, I welcomed him to Saudi Arabia to convalesce but would offer no such refuge to violent President Assad of Syria and have recalled our ambassador from Damascus. Uncertainties abound but I can assure you there won't be any more trouble in Bahrain since the Peninsula Shield, a coalition of twelve hundred troops from Arab Gulf nations, marched in.

I envision great prosperity and peace and freedom for the proud people of Saudi Arabia and, along with my large Royal Family – I'm one of thirty-seven sons of our first king – have offered the most generous gifts and concessions. For years we've been sending thousands of our brightest young people to study abroad and, indeed, now have more scholars in the United States than before 9/11. And you should certainly be aware that we've made a woman deputy education minister overseeing a new department for female students. We're supremely committed to higher learning and shall spend a quarter of our annual budget on education. We shall also improve our judiciary and business practices and spend billions to benefit the jobless and billions more for housing subsidies. We're responding to the needs of our people. And I believe we would've done so to this degree even if there hadn't been an ominous Arab Spring.

We love freedom and proudly announce that in 2015 women will, for the first time, be permitted to vote in local elections and run for those offices. We aren't ready to let them vote in the upcoming elections but they don't mind since they're ecstatic about the future.

They know they're going to be relevant. And by then, with divine assistance, they may even be able to drive to the polls.

In order to maintain this burgeoning petroleum paradise it's essential that the noble House of Fahd survive. And we know the United States agrees. That was my hand President George W. Bush was holding when I visited him in 2005, and he owed me since I'd kissed his ass after he ignored my advice not to attack Iraq in 2003. We naturally also adore President Barack Obama and have given his wife beautiful jewelry. She can't keep the gems but she'll always have the memories. Americans and Saudis have the same interests. We've got to eradicate terrorism. I'm appalled fifteen of the nineteen 9/11 hijackers were Saudis. Thankfully they're all dead. And so are many others whom we've tortured and publicly beheaded. We believe in security and justice.

And just like the Americans we're terrified the Iranians might acquire nuclear weapons. We can't let that happen. That's why I've urged the United States to strike Iran and kill the snake. We'll never be safe as long as it's coiled. We'd like to help fight the Iranians. We and the Americans were blood brothers during Operation Desert Storm in 1991. Maybe we will be again, this time in Iran. I'm afraid, however, that we won't be able to help in a major way since we must maintain a large national guard to protect our family and make sure the army doesn't misbehave like others we've seen.

Generals

egyptian
generals
clever
indeed
mubarak
in
jail
while
they
warm
bed

Obama Analyzes Opposition

Only to you I confess that nine percent unemployment and suffocating debt could make me a Hoover the Republicans pray for, but I shall most likely generate more work with a bill opponents can't bury. Of those loudest huffing Mitt Romney's a snore though bigger than opposing dwarves. Rick Perry can't debate and daily appears more reckless. Herman Cain made much pizza and bears a deep voice but no experience and wacky tax schemes even conservatives abhor. Michele Bachmann's already withered under testosterone. John Huntsman, my former ambassador to China, speaks keen Mandarin but his English decidedly fails to resonate, and there are other candidates you barely know who needn't be here discussed. Though people generally vote for president and not their mates I know Perry would help Romney in the South, and having left the Democratic plantation Cain would drain perhaps ten of my black ninety-six but Mitt may choose someone safer for the salivating task of attacking economic conditions beyond human control and that overshadow my manly drone strikes.

Assad Ponders Gaddafi

Eagerly I watch news for I'm a worldly gentleman and unlike some Arab leaders I understand how history works. I've studied films of Mussolini dragged in streets and hung upside down next to his girlfriend, and I've seen a noose placed around Saddam's neck, and I remembered them when Gaddafi, bloodied and horrified, was jerked from the hood of a truck and bulled away by a howling mob, and in the next video I studied his wounded head the rebels used to yank his body along hot dusty earth.

I'm not worried that'll ever happen to me. I'm not in Libya but Syria where security's much stronger and NATO's not bombing us. Surely you understand my wife's in England merely to relax, and even here we wouldn't worry she'll ever hang upside down like the Duce's girlfriend.

Gaddafi Curtain Call

a star I remain
dedicated to arouse
people coming to view
their leader still
handsome albeit
bruised and bloody
bearing some holes
stretched on old mattress
in vegetable freezer at
shopping center where
extended hours prevail

CHAPTER 10

Wall Street Bonus

what's a bonus
students ask and
i say used to be
extra money for
damn good job
now it's
millions for
dogs who
piss billions

Mitt Romney Perplexed

I'm confused my fellow Republicans don't simply coronate me since I'm the steadiest, most experienced and attractive, and richest primary candidate. Instead they throw feisty Michele Bachmann at me but she's too tiny to spot on stage, and gunslinger Rick Perry dashes into dodge and starts shooting himself in the ass, and next storytelling Herman Cain surges before he's revealed to be a groper and political dunce, and now recycled Newt Gingrich, ever blustery and unstable, is supposed to be ahead of me. I'm tired of conservatives saying I can't win because I waffle all the time and am boring. I plan to counter with something exciting but can't figure out what.

Death in North Korea

North Korean Cuisine

after scavenging
for grass and weeds
mr and mrs north korea
sell tv bicycle sewing
machine and furniture
and in empty apartment
consume each other
beneath portraits
of dear leaders

Kim Jong-Il

kim jong il
died of food
and alcohol
overdose on
nuclear train

Mourning

dear leader
we mourn
so hell
will take you

Urging North Koreans

stop crying
rip down
his likeness
and dance

Assad Welcomes Arab League

What arrogance, what ignorance my enemies in Syria and abroad daily show. They should understand I've given the Arab league permission to travel and observe my country and verify my regime is lawful, popular, and restrained.

True, I did promise to withdraw my security forces and was so doing in Homs and elsewhere when Al Qaeda terrorists, aided by a few traitorous government troops, attacked rightful authorities of Syria, forcing me to bombard in self defense.

The Arab league is quite trustworthy and will verify my words. I especially admire the mission leader, General Mohamed Ahmed al-Dabi, who secured Omar al-Bashir's regime in the Sudan, eliminating enemies of state. He'll recognize the same vermin here.

Rabid protestors seem unaware the Arab League is comprised of far more people like me than distant and hypocritical democrats who for generations have spat on Arab dignity and killed countless thousands of our people. I by contrast have eliminated no more than five thousand violent enemies of state and am confident skillful leadership will prevent my ever departing in an unfortunate manner.

Nuclear Engineers

We're quite special and secretive so can't tell but you may guess who recently splattered blood of fourth Iranian nuclear scientist in two years. Our magnetic bombs pushed onto cars by motorcyclists are getting better and this time also killed a bodyguard. Too bad in previous attacks one scientist and another's family survived.

We're only people in the Middle East morally and intellectually qualified to have nuclear power and know you fear Arabs or Persians with nukes. In our tiny nation God's always yearned for us to have, we can't risk mortal threats. We must have more living space and often hammer in annexation apartments while Free World picks its liberated nose.

Our victims have neither the right nor ability to strike back. That would be terrorism. We love denouncing terrorism. When we're terrorists we call it survival. We know Americans agree but worry Iranian parliament shouts death to America and might blow up their passenger planers. That would be too bad but we're quite special and worth it

2012

CHAPTER 11

Calling Martin Luther King

(Telephone lines were jammed on his birthday and I couldn't get through until the next day when he granted two minutes.)

George Thomas Clark – What do you think of Barack Obama?

Martin Luther King – Disappointing but better than George Wallace.

GTC – He got the U.S. out of Iraq.

MLK – Not until politically expedient.

GTC – He's going to get the U.S. out of Afghanistan.

MLK – But not until politically expedient.

GTC – He's trying to avoid war with Iran.

MLK – And will continue until not politically expedient.

GTC – What would you do now that things are much better and we have a black president?

MLK – I'd talk about poverty, the financial crisis, and the percentage of blacks in prison.

GTC – What about good things?

MLK – Only incumbents claim things are good. Civil rights leaders must be eternal candidates.

Martin Luther King: "Beyond Vietnam"

a million die
by 1966 day
i deliver "beyond
vietnam a time
to break silence"
declaring poverty
inevitable in "society
gone mad on war"
and still i see
america attacks
to feed "giant
triplets of racism
materialism and
militarism"

Perry to Romney

pardner
i told you
after that
debate
put yur
hand on me
again
i'll whup
yur ass
guaranteed
i ain't really
quittin
this race
just pushin
newt gingrich
up yurs

Romney Attacks in Florida

I know I shouldn't have been nice in a South Carolina alley fight with knife-wielding New Gingrich. Now in the Sunshine State I've got my switchblade at his throat for ethics violations that forced an unprecedented and disgraceful resignation as Speaker of the House.

Americans should also know Gingrich got worse serving as an insider lobbyist for federal mortgage insurer Freddie Mac, receiving one point six million bucks he should give back. He won't, though, because he's dishonest. I'm calling him out and ignoring intrusive demands I release income tax forms and explain why I slid modest sums into the Cayman Islands.

State of Union

I opposed the second Iraq war but today thank those who served and left the country ready to explode. We must also appreciate eruptions to come in Afghanistan, a war I campaigned to escalate, and eventually hope to end without resembling Lyndon Johnson or Richard Nixon. My American grandfather who fought for General Patton would be proud of me as would African Grandfather Obama who kicked many asses at work and home. Perhaps I should lead this nation in similar martial fashion.

Alas, I'm doomed to wearing a suit decorated by a flag pin rather than medals and am thus proscribed from throttling Wall Street bandits who've bilked America. Someday I'll pass laws to restrain them. And don't worry my key economic advisers are also thieves and insiders, that couldn't be avoided if I wanted to occupy and maintain my lovely oval office.

Thanks almost exclusively to my personal intervention, the U.S. auto industry has been saved and General Motors is selling more cars than anyone. They may not equal Japanese cars but brave customers are keeping industry out of the tank while we get tough on China with my new trade enforcement unit. We'll stop their pirating our software and intellectual property and use reclaimed funds to provide job training for countless unskilled workers whose votes I must have to hike taxes on tycoons like Mitt Romney.

If reelected I shall reform education by building an elite army of bold and creative teachers who must perform or be ejected into the masses of unemployed high school dropouts who next term I'll by law keep in class until they graduate or turn eighteen. They know I'm rough. Look how I've put more boots on the Mexican border than anyone and cut illegal crossings which, granted, fell along with U.S. jobs.

I'm celebrating a wave of change in the Middle East and preparing troops and the public for the next war in Iran. All options are on table to prevent bearded clerics from getting nuclear weapons. Iran better understand the United States with me in command is no longer in decline. We'll be able to maintain the best military in the world while saving a half-trillion dollars. George W. Bush made similar promises but couldn't deliver. I can. God bless my reelection campaign.

Love Immigrants

for hungry
hispanic floridians
newt gingrich
sautéed opponent
as anti immigrant
bon mitt responded
father's birthplace
mexico
and wife's father
from wales
making mitt
welsh mexican
an earthy patrician
who welcomes
strangers like
newt gingrich

CHAPTER 12

Israel Defends Settlements

don't
understand
why idiots
consider west
bank settlements
illegal how so
after we make
new laws
declaring them
legal
at which point
palestinians
illegally living
too near
our lawful land

Romney Cares for Poor

All politicians occasionally chew on toenails. That's what happened here. I misspoke and then my words were distorted. I really do care about poor, but don't worry too much because all forty-six million have safety net spreading almost fast as poverty.

Eternal Taliban

You'll never reliably read the Taliban's being uprooted from Afghanistan. Instead you'll be reminded I'm still pre-9/11 Mullah Omar whose zealots thrilled stadium crowds, stoning adulterers, lopping off thieves' hands, and taking our popular show into Pashtun farmland in south and east Afghanistan.

Now we're protected in Pakistan by the Inter-Services Intelligence agency helping me plot a comeback. Traitorous Afghans know most of them are being killed by the Taliban, not the United States, and we'll continue to detonate with impunity and preside as judges in mobile courts that warn: join us or die when America departs proclaiming victory through a foul mouth.

Muslim Analyst on Iran and the Nuclear Solution

Current doctrine in the United States, most of Europe, and many other places declares that Iran must not be permitted to acquire nuclear weapons or the purported Persian piranha will use them to strike the Israelis or blackmail them and the United States and ignite an arms race in the Middle East certain to result in at least regional Armageddon.

This analysis is racist and condescending and presumes nuclear incineration – or that delightful acronym MAD, mutually assured destruction – is not sufficiently severe to deter foreign savages who care not about preserving their civilizations.

Let us refute the forgoing nonsense by simply looking at the Twentieth Century. Nuclear weapons have been used but twice, by god-blessed America to end World War Two. The Soviet Union developed its own big bomb three years later, and for ensuing decades the two gorillas have refrained from nuclear attacks lest the other annihilate it with a counterstrike. China has likewise controlled itself since the mid-sixties. England and France are also nuclear armed but fond of survival. India and Pakistan frequently threaten each other but do not attack primarily because of deterrence. North Korea, a new wielder of nuclear weapons, has not, despite millions of starving citizens and primitive leadership, flirted with suicide.

Israel, long a nuclear nation, has at least restrained itself at the existential level, yet believes no other nation in the Middle East is intellectually or morally qualified to do so. That delusion is unsustainable and leads to this inevitability: either no one has nuclear weapons or any nation that wants them will someday develop them. If Iran gets a big bomb then so will Turkey, and if Turkey does then so will Egypt and Saudi Arabia and many others. And if Iran doesn't start this chain reaction, another nation will. That is frightening but less so than the United States and Soviet Union, once armed with forty thousand nuclear warheads apiece, glowering at each other. They've since become almost pacifistic, each reducing its arsenal to about ten thousand warheads.

We must live with dangerous potentialities, satisfied that nations can be trusted with nuclear weapons because nations can be identified and held accountable. And if a dirty bomb is slipped into terroristic hands? That can be precluded by an unequivocal commitment to Nuclear Sharia Law: he who passes such a weapon will lose his head.

More Bombings in Iraq

somewhere
saddam hussein
sneers at
george w bush
about sunni bomb
attacks on wobbly
u.s. built
sunni government
in texas
bush appalled
barack obama
letting his
raw nation
crumble
in white house
obama worries
bush and saddam
forming coalition

Red Light Rush

who's
whore
young
woman
advocating
funds
for
contraception
or
rush
limbaugh
splitting
cheeks
for
cash

Netanyahu Prays for Iran

Israel has the right to take unilateral action. We must master our own fate. We must control our own destiny. We must dominate the Middle East. We must attack Iran soon or the nuclear snake will strike us first. I say this looking right at the strange American president so unlike his predecessors. I say this believing that sanctions can't work and hoping they won't so the United States must act for us.

Assad Explains Siege of Homs

I've been reading international reports. People are saying I've sequestered myself with sycophants and yes men. They should be quiet and listen to the truth. I admit my opposition's a bit broader than initially perceived. Quite a few terrorist-infected Syrians don't understand the Assad dynasty must endure. To protect the country I've been forced to mass artillery and troops outside Homs, my third largest city, and shell the starving traitors. About three weeks later, after sending in troops, I delayed United Nations monitors until most corpses were removed from a rebellious neighborhood and spared our guests an unpleasant odor.

America to Afghanistan

we'll bomb
your weddings
and piss
on corpses
we'll burn
your korans
and invade
your homes
and shoot
children
at night
and keep
pretending
afghanistan
essential
till november
at least

Courtroom Defense of Robert Bales

In this military court, as counsel for the defense, I stand respectfully among fellow veterans of armed combat who understand, far better than any uninvolved civilian ever could, that my client, Sergeant Robert Bales, is not truly guilty of mass murdering civilians in Afghanistan. He cannot be, for Sergeant Bales is also a victim. He is a victim of war. He's a victim of barbarism without cease. He has been wounded and battered. He's been degraded and dehumanized. And, as such, he is forever ruined even if he does sit breathing in this courtroom today.

You are doubtless aware of the tragic progression that ultimately destroyed the soul of Robert Bales. He was a stockbroker who strove to better the financial and emotional lives of his clients. Then, after 9/11, that merciless strike at our American soul, an attack which killed some three thousand innocents, he, unlike millions who merely beat their chests, volunteered to defend his country. He volunteered to fight our enemies. He bravely stood between us and them.

Sergeant Bales first fought for a year in Iraq. As an expert sniper he silently eliminated adversaries before they could strike. He was wounded but did not surrender. He recovered and returned for another year of combat. In 2007 southern Iraq he and comrades killed two hundred fifty enemies while suffering not a single casualty. Afterward, Sergeant Bales spoke to journalists about his great pride in being one of the "good guys," the Americans who "differentiated between the bad guys and the noncombatants and then" warmly helped "the people that three or four hours before were trying to kill" them.

In time, while serving back in the United States, Sergeant Bales married and had two children and purchased a family home outside Seattle. Then he had to fight another year in Iraq. He suffered more wounds, physical and psychological. Only two years ago, riding in a vehicle that rolled over, he suffered a traumatic brain injury. I must tell my fellow warriors in this courtroom: Sergeant Robert Bales should not have been sent into battle again. He urgently desired to avoid further conflict and merely wanted what he had earned: a modest promotion to Sergeant E-7. That was denied, despite his long and many sacrifices for his country.

Instead, Sergeant Robert Bales was ordered to once again leave his wife and children and go to war, this time in Afghanistan. On his fourth tour Sergeant Bales, as ever, frequently took enemy fire, ministered to wounded comrades, and too often watched them die. He and his comrades seldom knew who the enemy was: the Taliban in the hills or "allies" in a village who pretended to be peaceful. The very March day the sergeant snapped, he saw a fellow soldier step on a land mine and lose his leg.

That night, about three a.m., as the sergeant has admitted, he crept off base and into a neighboring village and fired multiple rounds into people as they slept. Many were women and children. Then he set a number of bodies on fire. To this court I say: that wasn't Sergeant Robert Bales acting. How could he murder children? He is a father. No, Sergeant Bales was not the culprit. War itself is. War killed those people. What else do you expect in a war?

Confidential Legal Memo: What can we expect in the mass murder trial of Sergeant Robert Bales? As defense counsel I looked back at the 1970-71 trial of Lieutenant William Calley, accused of ordering the execution of one hundred four Vietnamese civilians in the hamlet of My Lai. He was convicted of murdering twenty-two and sentenced to life in prison. Patriots protested Calley was being mistreated. They accepted his explanation that he'd been ordered to destroy all enemies including unarmed men, women, and children. President Richard Nixon, and eighty percent of Americans polled, agreed. Nixon ordered Calley be placed under house arrest at Fort Benning, Georgia, where he served three and a half years before being released. Robert Bales cannot claim he was following orders, so will probably serve a few more years than Calley.

Shopping with Missus Assad

I'm so tired of terrorists ruining Syria and making it hard to visit my hometown London for real shopping. Now I must buy online and wait forever to get jewels, vases, Venetian glass, furniture, and crystal coated stilettos I can't find any suitable place to wear.

CHAPTER 13

Stand Your Ground

floridians
terrified
can't carry
guns at work
or in classrooms
but eagerly stash
in cars and carry
about everywhere
else to open fire
long as target's
only witness

Handbook for Vigilantes

Do not be a vigilante.

Take up wrestling or mixed martial arts if you want to test yourself.

If you cannot shake obsessions and paranoia about criminal adversaries, consider psychotherapy or becoming a real cop, though you will probably be found lacking. In that regard, do not push and curse a police officer (in 2005) and force him to arrest you.

If you cannot restrain yourself from becoming a vigilante, under the guise of being a volunteer neighborhood watch leader, do not presume that you have police powers. You do not. Read the handbook.

Do not inundate the police with trivial complaints.

Leave your gun at home.

You must not hound people you are suspicious of. That means do not chase shoplifters, real or imagined, or speed after drivers who may or may not have been driving recklessly before you horrified them, or follow pedestrians in your neighborhood, even if they're young black males.

When a police dispatcher tells you to stop following someone, obey the command. Qualified police officers are on the way.

Do not harass and ultimately pursue a skinny seventeen-year old like Trayvon Martin and then, one on one, face to face, get your ass kicked, and shoot the kid you'd been terrorizing, and then blame him for attacking you from behind, and hide behind self-defense claims you pray no living person can refute.

Conservative International Action Plan

We don't think the United States will soon cease having at least one war to fight, but we're getting worried. The ungrateful Iraqis just booted us because we insisted our soldiers receive judicial immunity. That's excruciating since we could've done more nation building and proselytizing. At least we're still battling the Taliban as well as our traitorous allies in Afghanistan but weak-on-defense President Obama and soft generals under his influence are scheming to skedaddle, perhaps as early as late next year. Maybe we can just move our troops over into Pakistan, which is a lot more dangerous, anyway.

If that doesn't work, and if Obama loses in November, I think we Republicans can convince all patriots that attacking Iran is necessary to destroy its nuclear weapons program. I hope they really have one. And I'm pretty sure they do. We don't want any more Saddam mass destruction deals. And while bombing Iran we should also go next door and hammer Bashar al-Assad in Syria. Everyone but the Russians and Chinese wants that bastard out.

Some are frightened considering life without war, but I'm not worried. Last weekend Al Qaeda attacked an army base in Yemen and killed about two hundred soldiers, decapitating some of them. Hell, if Al Qaeda's going to come out of its caves, compounds, and apartments and fight like men, then we sure as hell ought to invade Yemen. If we don't, they may hit your town next.

A few conservative pessimists think because of the Arab Spring and all the rumbling for democracy we may eventually run out of wars in the Middle East and have to find conflicts elsewhere. That will be easy. We need to expand our naval capacity in the Pacific Ocean so we can blockade the Chinese. Some say that would be dangerous, expensive, and unnecessary. The same chickens said that about Vietnam.

I'm also hoping Vladimir Putin keeps trying to smother democracy in Russia and back bad guys like Assad. I know better than to pray for a shooting war with the Russians, but a Cold War would be gratifying until something small and hot heats up.

Another Obama is Hitler Letter

The letter and email writers are always quite solemn as they rouse themselves and reactionary brethren with insipid historical analogies they think prove Barack Obama is striving to become the next Adolf Hitler and America will be doomed unless the nation responds to their cries for rebellion against tyranny. These self-admiring saviors are evidently unaware that if Obama were Hitler they wouldn't be publicly thrashing him. They'd be in Dachau or dead.

Rational observers must assume contemporary alarmists haven't studied Hitler's career or acquired even cursory knowledge of a man who killed fifty million people and whose primary regret was he couldn't continue the slaughter. What has Obama done to be compared to such a beast? According to one intrepid email philosopher, Obama and Hitler were both born in countries other than the ones they ruled and estranged from their fathers who at any rate died when they were young. I perhaps should've kept that long-deleted missive to offer more points I've forgotten except for their absurdity.

I'll be more specific about a worried conservative who recently signed his name to a letter to the editor in a Central Valley newspaper. He had been reading about William Shirer and his book "Rise and Fall of the Third Reich" in Smithsonian magazine. He didn't say if he'd read Shirer's long book. He's probably more comfortable reading short pieces about the book. At any rate, the letter writer was alarmed by the article's message that Germany had "delivered itself over 'to the dictates of one man.' (And) after reading that, it flashed through (his) head that we are living in a time which will, if left unchecked, destroy the foundation of America."

He next quoted Shirer that "contempt is not for Hitler so much as for the little men of Germany" who, he emphasized, "so readily acceded to the dictates of one man." Then he presented the horrifying question: "Is it happening here in America?" He thinks so because President Obama is trying to establish universal health care, which by inference the letter writer must consider a plot as diabolical as the Final Solution. "Where does the U.S. Constitution give one man the right to dictate health plans for the masses…?" he lamented. Actually,

Barack Obama cannot issue any such dictate. The Supreme Court, America's ultimate arbiter of constitutional issues, will decide whether the federal government can mandate that people buy health insurance. That's not how things worked in Nazi Germany, Herr Letter writer. And he should not worry that Adolf Obama is going to demand people "use contraceptives" or drive "green automobiles… and so on."

Before their programs are enacted, all presidents must get them passed by Congress, which has the power to fund or not. The Hitler-strangled Reichstag was first rendered impotent and then essentially nonexistent, quite different from Obama's Tea Party adversaries, in the House of Representatives, who stonewall and bellow much of the time. Don't worry, Hitler analogists, it will never be "impossible" for the "little men of America (to) stand up." The current president is an advocate of freedom. Ask the people of South Korea, where he recently visited to combat the tyranny and nuclear weaponry of North Korea. That, I assure you, Adolf Hitler would not be doing.

More American Love

don't know
how many
afghans
uncle sam's
gonna kill
for 9/11
but certain
there'll be
more photogenic
soldiers defiling
corpses still
not clear
if they'll pose
with kids
shot in bed

Israel Explains Settlements

don't palestinians
understand we must
keep legalizing outposts
and expanding settlements
can't stop till we've had
peace negotiations which
palestinians don't want
unless we cease building
and they'd have to be dumb
to think we'll ever do that

Assad's Guidelines

not afraid
of international
observers in syria
i simply want
them to see what
they should and
not talk to terrorists
who may be shot if
they look like they're
lying about me

Netanyahu Silent about Chief of Staff

As besieged but still restrained Prime Minister of Israel I can't say if I authorized Chief of Staff Benny Ganz to publicly guess that Iran won't build nuclear weapons and that its leaders are very rational. No matter what others say I know most Israeli leaders should insist Iranians want war and by so doing we'll someday prove we were right.

Obama in Afghanistan

In cool darkness at this military base, just before incredible dawn, some of you are wondering why I, like Alexander the Great, am riding a white horse and waving a sword. I do so not to boast or campaign but tell you in sacred tones that my sword is the head of Osama bin Laden and a beacon of my commitment to a prosperous and dignified Afghanistan that will never again be ruled by the Taliban, former host of Al Qaeda terrorists, most of whom, upon my resolute orders, have been obliterated.

It is the most painful regret of my life that I did not personally deliver the deadly blows, but I appear here today – atop Bucephalus – to assure you that I am both warrior and statesman and have ensured, even as American troops continue to withdraw, our Afghan allies are strengthening and will soon peak with three hundred fifty thousand troops poised to defend their country. The Taliban can be part of this but only if it severs relations with Al Qaeda. I believe the Taliban will respond favorably not only because it fears me but due to our recently-sanctified agreement with Afghanistan that guarantees for a millennium, if necessary, we are prepared to train indigenous allies and use our special operations to pounce on enemies inside and outside this troubled land. I also hope the neighboring Pakistanis, who so long hid Osama bin Laden, understand our unwavering concern. I know God understands. And He has blessed our troops and the United States of America.

CHAPTER 14

Obama v. Romney in Number$

what's difference
in presidential
candidates

barack obama
website offers
donor options
5-10-25-50-100
250-500-other

mitt romney
website offers
donor options
25-100-250
500-1,000
5,000-other

which provokes
bigger question
why are working
class whites
staunch republicans

Assad Justifies Bombardment

I'm not ashamed to tell you my Syrian forces unleashed artillery on the city of Houla. They had to. Terrorists, who've been attacking and planned to again, were hiding there. Any good commander would've pounded them. But I'm more humane than most. I ordered my troops to be restrained when they entered this hostile and dangerous place. And they followed orders but were quite traumatized. My enemies, an armed mob, had already stormed through and shot and stabbed civilians, more than half women and children, and then blamed the disfigured corpses on me. That's insulting; my army is professional. And, despite endless attacks upon me, I remain a man of honor. Otherwise, thousands more terroristic enemies of my presidency would've perished in recent months.

Romney Money Plane

I enjoy arranging Mitt Romney's fundraising forays. We land in Bakersfield early afternoon and roll in a police-escorted caravan of SUVs to a tree-hidden estate of the widow (now remarried) of one of two wealthy brothers, who both died in their fifties but had already built the world's largest producer of carrots. This is rarefied territory in Kern County, and that's what it takes to get close to Mitt. Don't smirk. Barack Obama doesn't visit modest homes, he passes the hat in George Clooney's castle. Mitt's just as handsome and urbane as those guys and knows how to attract the right people, those who can pay twenty-five thousand dollars to attend a private speech, ten thousand if they want their photo taken with the candidate, and fifty grand to join the cocktail party. The affair only lasts an hour and we're in town about two. We like to move fast. We've already been to Fresno this morning and now are headed to Los Angeles. We must keep bringing in money so we can elect a bold entrepreneur to replace that socialist in the White House and get big government off our backs.

Syrian Composer Speaks

My name's Malek Jandali. I compose classical music, play the piano in concerts around the world, and am an artist who loves everyone, though this Sunday afternoon, in the same Hammer Museum theater where I'll perform tomorrow, I'm not discussing international harmony; I'm talking about mass murder in Syria. The town where I was raised, Homs, does not exist anymore. President Bashar al-Assad ordered artillery units to pulverize the surrounded city before troops stormed in and killed many of the survivors. Assad believes in destroying symbols of freedom. He learned that from his father, Hafez al-Assad, who in 1982 massacred about forty thousand opponents in the town of Hama. Those that Assad spared, some women and children, were dispersed to spread fear throughout Syria.

Can you imagine the United States armed forces bombing Los Angeles for sixteen months as Bashar al-Assad has battered Syria? That's why there's an eternal brain drain. Artists and other creative people are either in prison or exile. Those who remain are afraid to express their feelings. Syrians must adapt to survive. They have to become "professional liars." Every morning at school students and teachers praise the dictator, and then at home denounce him.

When I left to study music at North Carolina School of the Arts, I still believed I would someday return to Syria because I'd miss family and home, but I tasted freedom, respect, and opportunity and decided to stay. I'm a U.S. citizen now and accustomed to speaking candidly. That's why I'm telling you the Free Syrian Army has no tanks and planes and few rifles and is thoroughly outgunned by the modern army of Assad. I'm not asking the United States to put troops in Syria but to establish a no-fly zone and contribute weapons and food; as the most powerful nation in the world, the U.S. is obligated to do something.

The Syrian people are ready to finish off Assad. They're ready to be free. Dictatorships will soon be impossible. The social media are revealing the truth. Facebook and cell phones turn millions into journalists poised to report and take pictures. I understand the dangers in a very personal way. Two days after I performed at the White House for President Barack Obama, Assad's goons beat my elderly parents and warned them their American son better stop making trouble.

Gun Enthusiast Explains Lessons of Aurora

We gun-cradling Americans are appalled by that mass murderer in Aurora, Colorado and just as upset by pink-panties liberals who're still using this tragedy to yelp for more gun control. Folks, we need less control, not more. It's real simple. If adults in that movie theater had been packin', they'd have blown away the misfit James Holmes after he'd shot only a few people, and a dozen lives would've been saved and dozens spared serious wounds. Don't tell me assault guns are to blame. Criminals will always get any weapon they want. It's our American duty to ensure decent citizens always bear the tools of justice.

A Drone for You

Forget those primitive large drones that fire hundred-pound missiles into wedding parties and drop five-hundred-pound bombs on families. They're passé and about to be replaced by sleek Switchblades about the size of model planes armed with six-pound bombs that can reliably fly into terroristic trousers without blowing up nearby people and buildings.

Regrettably, the Pentagon cannot sell you the Deluxe Switchblade but next week we will make available, for only a million dollars apiece, the super-accurate Suburban Switchblade that will taser anyone you select, be it a nasty spouse, insulting coworker, or reckless motorist.

Warning: The Pentagon is not legally or financially responsible if you improperly use your Switchblade.

CHAPTER 15

South Chicago Man in Quito

At a conference in Quito for people, generally from the United States, who want to learn about opportunities for cultural adventure and less expensive living in Ecuador, I sat in a padded chair, waiting for a prominent local attorney to appear and offer advice about obtaining visas and buying property in his country. Next to me stood a rather plump and haggard fellow who asked, "Where are you from?"

"Bakersfield, California. And you?"

"South of Chicago."

"Is that near where Barack Obama lives?"

"I live further south, in another county. Obama's an evil man. I learned that years ago. My wife had a terrible experience with him before he was famous, about the time he became a U.S. Senator."

I thought oh no. Did the young Obama insult her? Did he brush her off? Did he grope her?

"What happened?"

"I got home one night and immediately saw my wife was extremely upset. People were gathered around her, trying to comfort her. I asked, 'Honey, what's the matter?'"

She said, "Barack Obama shook my hand this evening and every hair on my arms stood on end. The man is evil, and he's going to be the President of the United States."

"If he made such a bad impression, why did she think an unknown politician would go on to become president?"

"She just knew," he said. "And Obama is evil."

The Quito attorney then rescued me.

Alarmed by "2016 Obama's America"

I'm one knowledgeable conservative, having lived all my life in Bakersfield and spent hours a day listening to Rush Limbaugh, Sean Hannity, and other great political analysts, and all my friends in the oilfields think like I do, and we understand Barack Obama is the most dangerous man in American history. But, I gotta tell you, we didn't know the worst until we and our wives got together last night, went to the theater, and watched an extraordinary documentary: "2016 Obama's America." Usually, I don't watch documentaries because they're made by liberals and very boring and I like movies with lots of fights and explosions and car crashes and potty jokes. That kind of entertainment is what conservative working people love all over the country, and especially in Bakersfield which, if you ignore media attacks about us having dirty air and lots of high school dropouts and unemployment, is the greatest place to live.

Anyway, we were blown away by evidence that Barack Obama is planning to destroy America. The brilliant director, Dinesh D'Souza, has it all figured out. In order to understand Obama, you've got to go back to the independence of Kenya. Dinesh understands historical kind of stuff because right out of college he was hired to give advice to President Ronald Reagan, and knows all about Obama since they were born the same year, both attended Ivy League schools and graduated the same year, and even married the same year. Early in the movie Dinesh makes the point that Obama came out of nowhere, no one knew anything about him, and he got elected because he promised hope. What white guy would've been allowed to move into the White House just two years after he left the Illinois state legislature?

Instead of giving us hope, Barack Obama has presided over the United States losing forty percent of its wealth since 2007. Okay, some of that was the last part of George W. Bush's administration, but most of it was Obama's. We should've known right away he was trouble. He came into the White House and removed the bust of Winston Churchill, the great British defender against the Nazis and a man determined not to "preside over the dissolution of the British Empire." Obama also insults our English-speaking brothers by backing

Argentina's efforts to get back the Falklands Islands even though the British have had them a long time and reconquered them after Argentine aggression in 1982. We also have to wonder why Obama keeps blocking U.S. oil drilling while encouraging many developing countries to drill, drill, drill. We wonder too why Obama used U.S. force to stop genocide in Libya but not in Syria. Why hasn't he done more to stop the Iranians from getting nuclear weapons? His sanctions won't work. He doesn't care. He's against Israel and takes the Palestinian position that Israel should quit annexing the West Bank. I know God wants the Israelis to own the West Bank.

Dinesh D'Souza points out that Barack Obama's drunken father, Barack, Sr., who killed a man in one car accident and lost both legs in another, and abused some of his wives and children, is the key to the president's anti-American behavior. His mother, Ann, often praised his father and created tension between Americanism and Africanism. Then, when Ann married an Indonesian, Lolo, and moved to his country, along with Barack, the youngster was exposed to more anti-colonialism. Dinesh, who's from India, understands some of this resentment. But he can't comprehend why Ann fantasized about her former husband, Barack, Sr., who never lived with her and abandoned her and the infant Barack, while resenting Lolo because he supported her by working for an American-owned oil company. She sent Barack to Hawaii to live with his leftist grandparents. The boy no doubt resented his mother sending him away and used that as an excuse to get angry about what he considered the illegal U.S. annexation of Hawaii.

I'll bet Sarah Palin has seen this movie and wasn't surprised to learn that Barack Obama began hanging out with terrorists when he was a teenager in Hawaii. His mentor in those days was a communist poet and journalist named Frank Marshall Davis. The FBI sure kept an eye on that guy. By the time Obama graduated from high school in 1979 he was probably already a communist sympathizer. Going to Occidental and Columbia for two years each, and later in the 1980s being a community organizer, no doubt further radicalized him. By the time he made his pilgrimage to Africa in 1987, he was anxious to embrace Africanism and reject Americanism and honor his father, who had visited him only once, in 1971, before dying in a 1982 drunk-driving accident

I loved Dinesh's interview with the president's much younger half brother, George Obama. Despite living in a ghetto and smelling of alcohol, George put everything in perspective, noting that Kenya was once on par with Malaysia and Singapore but now far behind the Asian tigers because they had embraced help from whites while Kenya rejected, and sometimes slaughtered, whites. George also points out that South Africa can thank whites for being more advanced than Kenya. That's why Barack Obama doesn't help his half brother get out of the slums: George doesn't worship at the altar of Barack, Sr. and others who blame all the world's problems on whites and colonialism.

Barack the son agrees with his father that the only way to control capitalists is by burdening them with high taxes. That's communistic and anti-American, and not surprising when you consider the future president moved from Frank Marshall Davis to many other radicals and terrorists. His Chicago buddy Bill Ayers, like Osama bin Laden, attacked targets in the United States. His Harvard law professor Roberto Unger was and is a raving socialist, but today even he opposes Obama being reelected because he believes the president has not been progressive, in other words not radical enough. And you know about Jeremiah Wright, Obama's pastor for twenty years and the man who presided at his marriage to Michelle. Wright hates whites and loathes America, the nation where he became a wealthy man.

Barack Obama is just like the guys he hung out with. He wants to make America impotent while building up former colonial nations. He wants to reduce our nuclear weapons and eventually disarm us in a dangerous world. He wants to increase our deficit, which has grown much more under him than any under previous president, even George W. Bush. And of course he wants to raise taxes. He wants the United States to be a socialist state that withdraws from its international obligations. He wants to pretend U.S. power is not crucial in restraining many vicious forces around the world. Look at Dinesh's clever map, like a 1950s map of spreading communism. On this map Middle Eastern countries, those falling dominos, become radical Islamist states and will soon form the United States of Islam, which Barack Obama will love.

My buddies and I, all big-gutted and happy in white T-shirts, and our wives and everyone else in the theater applauded when the movie ended, and that doesn't happen often. Another Bakersfield friend I hadn't seen came up and said, "I'm glad you're here to see the Traitor in Chief."

Romney's Preparations for Republican Convention Speech

(Mitt Romney lectured his speechwriting staff two nights before his acceptance speech. This transcript was secretly recorded by a devious insider.)

For God's sake don't let me prominently mention I was Governor of Massachusetts. You know they'd tie Romneycare to Obamacare, and accuse me of being the moderate governor of a liberal state. They'll do that, anyway, but let them do so at their convention not ours.

My job is to convince Americans they doubt our children will have a better future. We were promised hope and change. Instead, President Barack Obama has delivered despair and debt and unemployment. I wish he had succeeded. Then the most exciting moment wouldn't have been when the misguided majority voted for him.

President Obama's problem is that he has no business experience. You can't be a great president unless you've made millions in business. Maybe that hasn't historically been true, but it's true now. That's why Obama attacks success. He resents those who've done well and wants Americans to feel the same negative way.

That's very strange. The United States needs jobs. One in six Americans is living in poverty, yet Obama preaches he's trying to heal the planet. I promise that I'm going to help your family. While the President wants to keep raising taxes and choking off jobs, I want to lower taxes – not for my benefit or that of my fellow elites – but to enable the ablest to use their creativity to create jobs. That's what I did at Bain Capital. I made companies more efficient so they could hire more people. Those that were inefficient had to be closed. That's how the free market system works. A socialist like Obama doesn't understand that.

He also doesn't understand energy. His assaults on coal and gas and oil will send energy and manufacturing jobs to China. Write that down. That's definitely going in my speech. He also wants to weaken our military. We may spend more on defense than all, or almost all, the other nations of the world combined, but that's not enough. We're Americans. That's something else birth-certificate-challenged Obama doesn't comprehend. And he won't have to after I beat him in November.

Then we'll be able to spend all we want because I'll create twelve million new jobs in five steps: I'll make us energy independent; I'll give our fellow Americans the job skills they need today; I'll forge new trade agreements that favor America, and when any other nation cheats there'll be unmistakable consequences; I'll ensure entrepreneurs that their investments in America will not vanish because I'm going to balance the budget. That doesn't make me sound like budget-balancing Bill Clinton, does it? Don't let me mention his name. And don't let me utter the words George W. Bush, either. I had a fifth point, too, didn't I? Of course. I'll champion small business, America's engine of job growth.

I know business and economics. And I also believe in the sanctity of life. I don't have to say I was pro-choice as a governor who now, for political expedience, will struggle to overturn Roe v. Wade. I will as well affirm my belief in the institution of marriage. I don't have to mention that marriage must exclude homosexuals. We all understand. Republicans wouldn't want marriage besmirched by them, and neither would I. I believe too strongly in the dignity of women to permit assaults on the family. Every American should know that my mother ran for the Senate and that I hired many women for important posts when I was Governor of Massachusetts. Don't worry, we'll attract more female voters that way than we'll lose by once mentioning that northeastern state. Women will also approve when I stress that my wife Ann had a harder job than mine. She raised five boys who frequently screamed at the same time.

We're not only less secure morally and financially than when Barack Obama became President, we're less secure physically. Iran is more a threat because Obama has failed to stop its nuclear weapons development. His sanctions aren't effective. He's also thrown bastions of democracy like Israel under the bus while easing sanctions on communist Cuba and going soft on a resurgent and dangerous Russia led by Vladimir Putin.

No reasonable American can possibly conclude that he or she is better off today than four years ago. Barack Obama and Jimmy Carter are unique incumbents in that regard. I don't think I'll need to mention Ronald Reagan, though I'd be proud to.

Limbaugh Offers Tips to Obama

Folks, I'm not a traitor to conservatism, I'm an American patriot and proud to tell you that if President Barack Obama secretly whisked me to the White House and admitted he'd given an excuse-ridden and "embarrassing" speech at the Democratic National Convention, and that he was doomed to become another one-term Jimmy Carter unless he immediately responded to my counsel, I would agree on condition that within forty-eight hours we release a video of my design. This celluloid tour de force would be received and vastly covered as news, rather than free advertising, and help us overcome the loaded wallets of Mitt Romney's backers

A transcript of my proposed video follows:

Rush Limbaugh – Mr. President, I did not mean that Sandra Fluke was literally a slut because she wanted government-funded birth control.

Barack Obama – I understand that, Rush. If she wants to light up the sheets, she and her many male companions should reach for their wallets.

RL – I think real women appreciate your position since most currently pay for their contraceptives or insist that their lawful husbands practice coitus interruptus.

BO – That's right. We must rid our national psyche of this notion that government, and particularly welfare, can take care of matters that beef-eating, entrepreneurial Americans should handle themselves.

RL – I know you believed that your stimulus packages and other economic efforts saved the country from an even greater fiscal calamity, but aren't you ready to admit you could've responded more effectively?

BO – I am, indeed. Though I still believe in my deft efforts to stimulate, I've recently concluded that tax cuts even deeper than those already in place, and named after my honorable predecessor, George W. Bush, would've invigorated the economy by encouraging our wealthiest citizens to invest their tax bounty in jobs-producing endeavors. Then we could've begun to lower the deficit that was created by those who cater to freeloaders.

RL – The highlight of your convention speech occurred when you vowed to maintain the United States military as the mightiest arsenal in the history of mankind.

BO – That I shall certainly do. I plan to continue attacking Al Qaeda all over the world and to kick ass in Afghanistan two more years and bombard Iran if they don't unequivocally destroy their nuclear weapons. I'd also like to return to a Cold War standoff with the Russians to ensure they don't try to regain their Soviet empire. I know I said otherwise at the convention, but that was for weak-kneed liberals.

RL – The libs will have to stick with you.

BO – I just pray, several times a day, but not pointed toward Mecca, that conservatives will quit calling me a traitor and the enemy and give me four more years.

RL – Are you prepared to state that life begins at conception and to fight to overturn Roe v. Wade.

BO – I'm ready to concede that a fetus is alive. Let the people and the state supreme courts decide the issue of legality.

RL – Bravo. And let the people choose their own health care providers, even in old age. Medicare's a drag on the economy.

BO – Indeed, we must set up private accounts that motivate the most talented doctors, for the most generous fees, to minister to our seniors. We're a nation of strivers and dreamers and risk-takers, and need that competitive spirit in health care as well as education and government, which not only can't solve all our problems but, as President Ronald Reagan said, is in fact the problem.

RL – So you no longer believe that citizenship is some nam-by-pamby process of diffident people clinging to each other while preaching they're doing so for future generations.

BO – Certainly not. United States citizenship is about owning a gun, starting a business, hiring people, firing people, making more money, being in a sacred union between a man and a woman, going to church where there's a patriotic pastor, and always backing any president who says we've got to attack the enemy. That's why we're the greatest nation on earth. God bless you, Rush, and may God bless these United States of America.

Mitt Romney Frames New Middle East

You already know our soon-to-be-ex President Barack Obama apologized for American values, principally free speech and a dimwit's right to make a bad film insulting the Prophet Muhammad, before and after our Libyan consulate was attacked in Benghazi and Ambassador J. Christopher Stevens and three others were murdered. And soon we saw how President Obama's weakness emboldened other terrorists to assault our embassies and properties in Egypt, Yemen, Tunisia, Lebanon, and many other places in that unholy morass – excepting Israel – that's quaintly but deceptively called the Middle East. Truthfully, that part of the world is a nightmarish threat, and as the next President of the United States I vow to control it, and will now be quite specific in articulating how to do so.

First, I will spend what we must on defense. President Obama has gutted our armed forces, never mind that we still spend far more than any other nation ever has. Our needs are greater. We have commitments all over the world. People need us and love us. Let's start with Libya. This dessert wasteland would be insignificant if not for oil but oil it has so we must immediately station more troops there to protect energy and surround our embassy and other diplomatic missions with American military personnel ready to fire and kill before any gathering mob has a chance to attack. This doctrine of preemptive strike clearly also applies to every country in the Middle East. My bold moves will also be political in nature. I would've saved our Egyptian ally of thirty years, President Hosni Mubarak, rather than let him be hogtied and replaced by the Muslim Brotherhood and its new President Mohammed Mursi, who on his knees doubtless prayed for our demise while fellow terrorists looted our embassy in Cairo. American troops are also clearly needed in Egypt.

Really, that is the fundamental point. We need more troops everywhere. We must protect ourselves from the festering masses who, quite temporarily I'm sure, have forgotten we're their saviors. We'll teach them. I understand spiritual salvation. For two years I was a Mormon missionary. But let me promise I won't try to pry those people from their religion of hatred, oppression, and terrorism. I believe in freedom of religion, and will help them protect their sacred beliefs, and do so by maintaining an American full nelson. This technique will work on the Iranians. We may have to bomb them in order to secure Israel's nuclear monopoly in the region, but after we've crushed them they too will embrace us like the liberated Libyans and Iraqis and almost-liberated Afghans. Name a country, as long as its one not strong enough to really hit back, and I guarantee if we kill enough bad guys the remaining good guys will love us.

Barack and Michelle Audio Soars on Internet

My outlook must be unaligned with that of the masses for I here certify most television programs and commercials are insipid and only morons watch reality shows, which I've done but once, when compelled to write about the domestic activities of presidential aspirant Sarah Palin. On a recent night, while watching the muscular students of Stanford grind and pound the favored future pros of USC, I sensed the onset of major depression, invoked by the barrage of inane sales pitches, and clicked to another channel which, thankfully, I thought, was offering an interview with Barack and Michelle Obama on Entertainment Tonight.

I should have been wary of the programming source as well as the interviewer, a cocktail-lounge blonde whose fatuous and prurient questions made Palin seem profound. What most distressed me was that the Obamas responded to the interviewer's repeated allusions to romance, and cuddled and cooed onscreen in a manner that demonstrated desperate desire to win reelection in November, and, more alarmingly, to embrace right there.

When their lips joined and hands began to probe regions south of the shoulders, I sensed television and political history were about to manifest. And it would have without the decency of the camera operator who kept his instrument pointed straight ahead and thus above the Obamas after they wrestled each other to the ground. As viewers examined empty chairs, they heard the first lady exhort and the president roar, and that audio has already received more than two hundred million hits and propelled the incumbent, who'd guarded but a slender advantage, to a ten-point lead over his less passionate challenger Mitt Romney who, we should emphasize, can likewise respond with his lovely wife, and perhaps not limit access to the mere auditory.

Assad Battles Terrorists

During my daily prayers I often humbly ask what I should do to save Syria. At least five thousand foreign terrorists have joined domestic criminals and are trying to destroy this wonderful land, over which my late father, a great and wise leader unjustly accused of mass murder, and I have ruled for two generations.

I cannot abandon my fellow Syrians now. Our enemies, who've long attacked vulnerable places around the country, are now clawing toward our heart, in Damascus. They're in the southern part of the city and planting bombs in schools. They say that's necessary because my troops and militias use the grounds to bombard nearby neighborhoods where they hide prior to attacking me again.

That's a lie. Everything they say is a lie. I wouldn't damage or destroy tens of thousands of schools and homes and force refugees to use classrooms as homeless shelters. Only terrorists do that. They're also ruining our power stations, factories, and pharmaceutical labs, leaving citizens without electricity and vital medications. Meanwhile, they're looting farms and disrupting transportation. This winter we'll face critical food shortages. What should I do?

I must fight these murderous enemies of mankind. I must fight as ruthlessly as they fight. They're attacking our hospitals yet accuse me of using medical care to lure wounded enemies into snares. I'd never behave that way or traumatize our children, which is precisely what the terrorists do when they torture and kill parents and other relatives as little ones watch. I must stop these atrocities. They're not merely attacks on Syria; they're assaults on international civilization. That's why I cannot accede to the United Nations demand that I cease firing and start stepping toward the exit. Where would I go? They just attacked military headquarters about a mile from my home.

Death Sentences in Iraq

I am a university student in Iraq and want to be rich so have decided to study criminal law. We need lots of skillful defense attorneys. The ones we have now evidently need more training. Twenty-one of their clients were executed one day last year and another five died two days later. Around a hundred have been executed so far this year and another two hundred officially await the end. Unofficially, everyone believes totals are much higher.

I want to study these cases but the government releases little except corpses. I know some of those executed had been accused of murder but in Iraq there are about fifty capital offenses and no one outside ironclad courtrooms has details. I'd investigate but it's dangerous to interfere. From Turkey exiled Vice President Tariq al-Hashemi wrote to President Jalal Talabani that the nation should stop its arbitrary executions. A week later al-Hashemi was charged with killing two Shia officials and sentenced to death in absentia. He probably had a bad lawyer if he had one at all. That didn't matter, though, since he couldn't have had what most would consider a trial.

The United Nations and others complain about Iraqi injustice but are reminded American soldiers were banished and the government must provide security in a nation where hundreds are shot or blown up in streets. No doubt some bad people were responsible but they still deserve vigorous legal representation. And one thing we've learned, from survivors and their families, is many people are detained and tortured and torture is used to determine guilt or innocence. That surely will change.

CHAPTER 16

Romney Pummels Obama in First Debate

Federal prosecutors are now privately detailing charges that will soon be officially released. As a special agent for the FBI I have decided I must not wait so today tell you this: for two decades and more I've chased and usually captured terrorists, murderers, spies, kidnappers, bank robbers who used guns, pens, or computers, and many other wretches, but never have I uncovered a more insidious crime than that committed by Mitt Romney, and coconspirators to be identified, on the night of October third before and during his first debate with President Barack Obama.

Sixty million viewers in America demanded to know: what happened to the formerly charming and inspiring Obama? After several studies of our optically-enhanced film of the proceeding, I figured it out. Click on this link, which makes hundreds of times larger a speck on Romney's right hand, supposedly offered in fellowship before the debate, and you will note the head of a micro-needle used to drug the President of the United States before he began rhetorical defense of his title.

Romney and his henchmen couldn't risk the president fainting on the spot or instantly becoming incoherent. No, guided by diabolical chemists, they injected Obama with a moderate but devastating dosage of zonkola, which allowed the victim to open the debate as if unaffected, and state that he had rescued a nation on the precipice of another Great Depression, and the most dangerous financial crisis since then, by stimulating the economy, saving the auto industry, and creating five million jobs in the private sector. No one at this point was suspicious or alarmed.

Governor Romney responded that more of the same Obama policies would not work. Instead, he, the sagacious Mitt Romney, would right away make the nation energy independent and create four million new jobs, open up trade and crack down on China, the new Asian bogeyman, ensure that people have skills required to succeed, balance the budget, and champion small business.

Rather than demand to know how Romney, Santa Claus and the Easter Bunny would team to bring this about, Obama groggily began to talk about education, twice complimented Governor Romney for agreeing with him that the corporate tax rate was too high and the nation had to boost energy production, and, yawning, said the centerpiece of the challenger's plan was a five trillion dollar tax cut. A less-intoxicated Obama could have defended this position, but on his night he essentially applied blood to his throat and thrust it at Romney who rebuked the president for saying he had any such plan.

While Obama shrank behind his lectern, Romney looked authoritatively at him, and lectured that presidential policies had crushed the middle class by lowering their income. He called it the economy tax, and it continues to be crushing. Obama seemed crushed and ready to go home. He should've feigned a gastric disorder. He could've fallen to the canvas and at least taken an eight count. Instead, he ate Romney's next accusation of crushing something else, in this case the coal industry. Rather than counterattacking, Obama mumbled and frowned and bumbled as his handlers considered calling 911.

It would've been better to leave Romney alone on stage as he, the man who lurched to the right of Republican-primary reactionaries Newt Gingrich, Rick Perry, and Michele Bachmann, spontaneously transformed himself into Everyman America, a moderate savior of the middle class. Instead, Obama stayed and was visible to the nation as Romney promised not to raise taxes on the middle class and accused him of having a plan that would raise each person's taxes by four grand. Romney also vowed to lower taxes for small businesses and the little guys and thereby get millions more people hired. That was his plan. Obama's was trickle down government.

Beginning another sentence with "well," Obama wearily denied that Romney's plan would work and said that he, the president, had lowered small business taxes 18 times and that under his plan 97 percent of small businesses would not see their taxes go up. Romney, who should've been tested for uppers and performance-enhancing drugs, announced that those top-three-percent of businesses the president wants to squeeze are the very businesses that employ half – half – of all the people who work in small businesses.

Holding onto the ropes, Obama said Romney's massive-tax-cut approach had been tried in 2001 and 2003 and the result was the slowest job growth in 50 years. Romney again scolded the president for accusing him of planning a five trillion dollar tax cut. That wasn't his plan. He planned to eat Obama for dinner. After applying ketchup, he promised to put people back to work and avoid the horror of 32 million people on food stamps in 2009 increasing to 49 million this year. Obama buried chin in chest as his shoulders heaved.

Since the president didn't howl no mas or grab the challenger around the neck, Romney continued hurling haymakers. He was going to get rid of ridiculous Obamacare health care that wasn't really like his plan in 1990's Massachusetts. He didn't pay for his plan by borrowing money from China and doubling the national deficit. Obama staggered and whispered he did what he did because he inherited two wars paid for on a credit card. Raising taxes kills jobs, Romney countered. Since he's the personification of more jobs, he also represents more revenue and doesn't want the United States to become another Spain, spending 42 percent of its economy on government. Since the U.S. is now paying that amount, Obama must want America to become another Spain.

Almost out on his feet, but maintaining the instincts of a schoolmarm, Obama bemoaned tax breaks for big companies, bad guys who ship jobs overseas. Popping the presidential snout, Romney noted that tax breaks for oil companies amounted to only $2.8 billion a year, a pittance next to the $90 billion in breaks the president had given to solar and wind geeks. Romney said a friend had told him that Obama doesn't pick winners and losers, he only picks losers. Rather than defend himself, Obama in his silence seemed to be asking the challenger to keep chewing on his ass.

This Romney did, accusing Obama of cutting $716 billion from Medicare. The president's response was chopped up with "And – ... For – for – so if you're – if you –" and other sleep-inducing constructions. Obama did land a soft jab against voucher-craving Romney by noting Medicare administrative costs are lower than those in private care; few were moved by that relevant but wonky response.

Not merely intoxicated by the challenger's zonkola, perhaps paid for by Obamacare, the president must have been stunned when Mitt Romney suddenly transformed himself into a great regulator.

Regulation is essential. But regulation can be excessive. The last four years of regulation has hurt the country. Romney knows what kind of regulation will protect not only the big-money boys, but the little guys, Mitt's new buddies. Most of them by now resented what Obama roused himself to utter: lightly-regulated stock market, real estate, and banking corporations had recklessly ruined the economy and if you think there was too much insight on Wall Street then Romney's your candidate.

Polls already indicate Romney is the new choice of many voters. They won't recall most of Obama's lines. They'll remember Romney's charge that three-quarters of businesses say Obamacare hurts them and that the president is not fighting for jobs. The president failed to deny that but did say he's not trying to take away insurance from anyone who has it. He just wants the millions who don't have coverage to get it and for 18 percent less through Obamacare than private care. Like a guy who's taken too many punches from a bully, Obama blessed his attacker, complimenting Romney for getting along with Democrats in Massachusetts. Romney agreed he'd done a great job, established a model for the nation, and hadn't raised taxes. Obama said he'd used the same health-care advisors as Romney, who soon slapped him with the admonition that the federal government should not take over health care.

Indolent President Obama said Governor Romney doesn't think we need more teachers. Romney replied that he loved great schools, and education in Massachusetts, where he last governed six years ago, ranks number one in the nation. Within a minute he'd again segued into food stamps – 47 million of those Obama-backed moochers – and bemoaned that 23 million were out of work. Those numbers are more startling than the one a benumbed Obama responded with – Romney wants to cut the education budget up to 20 percent. The challenger bridled, quieted the hapless moderator, Jim Lehrer, and told Obama he was entitled to his own airplane and his own house, but not his own facts. He, Mitt Romney, was not going to cut education. And he was still darn sorry the president had thrown $90 billion into green energy, run by incompetents who'd contributed to Obama's campaigns, instead of using the money to hire two million teachers.

In closing, Obama sleepwalked through a sappy story about a middle-aged mother going back to school to inspire her daughter, and saying Governor Romney probably agrees that's he's been an imperfect president. Romney ended his 90-minute onslaught by telling voters that more Obama means their incomes will continue to come down while prices go up, and if he, Mitt Romney, is president, there will be more jobs and lower health care costs.

Backstage, minutes after again shaking Mitt Romney's treacherous hand, Barack Obama collapsed. He should've been permitted to sleep it off. Instead, he was revived, and into the camera he said, "I'm not lethargic, I'm relaxed. I'm not frigid, I'm cool. I'm not a masochist, but sometimes I enjoy being punched."

Ambassador's Father

father of
u.s. libyan
ambassador
chris stevens
says abhorrent
to politicize
son's death
in presidential
campaign

Afghan Trap: 1982 and 2012

Out back in the storage room my hands became gritty with ancient dust as I pried through files of light brown clips, seeking boxing articles for possible use in an upcoming book. I found the candidates but was most stirred by a column I wrote, "Russia Bogged Down in Afghanistan," in late 1982. Before starting to read I decided to substitute United States and Americans for every reference to the Soviet Union and Russians. With a few other minor alterations, this is the result:

The tunnel was dark and packed with buses and trucks and no one in the West knows exactly what happened after the explosion but this much is certain: a large gasoline tanker plowed into another vehicle and an inferno erupted and burned hundreds to death and killed hundreds more who tried to breathe smoke-shrouded air. This accident – or sabotage, perhaps – was caused by the war in Afghanistan and symbolized the futility of a large foreign nation trying to impose its will on a small, backward country.

Many of the dead were young American soldiers riding in convoys in the Salang pass seventy miles north of Kabul when the crash occurred. The majority of them believed what their leaders had told them: citizens of Afghanistan want and need American assistance to protect themselves from aggression. The American soldiers weren't told what many of the Afghan civilians who died with them in the tunnel already knew. A democratic government could not survive in Afghanistan without massive intervention. But instead of establishing Western-style security in Afghanistan, the Americans have in fact ensnared themselves in a seemingly endless confrontation where opposition is fierce and chances of victory are minimal.

The White House apparently doesn't realize that its criticism of Soviet involvement in Afghanistan also applies to itself. No matter how much sophisticated military hardware is deployed against an agrarian, lightly industrialized nation, the native people still cannot be forced to accept an unpopular and inept government. The Americans planned to subjugate the Afghans with relative impunity but their fantasies were based on false historical premises in a land where tribesmen tenaciously resist invaders. Sometimes captured American soldiers are executed and then mutilated and taken to roads where their comrades inevitably see how the mujahidin wage war.

The American model of nation building cannot succeed in a fundamentally different environment in Afghanistan. Anthony Arnold of the Russian Hoover Institute wrote, "The American Indians and their territories, fought over, conquered, and occupied by great powers for generation after generation, have been more or less accustomed to the experience of being dominated. Whatever their true feelings, considerations of sheer survival have dictated some measure of caution in dealing with large conquerors. This is not true of Afghanistan, where the resistance fighter and his forbearers have never in tribal memory been occupied by foreigners excerpt for the briefest interludes, where there is little of economic value to lose by fighting, where organizations (aside from the family/tribe) are almost nonexistent, and where the basic units of opposition are single, indomitable individuals, instead of malleable groups."

Despite killing thousands of resistance fighters – and civilians – with sophisticated weapons, the United States is still far from achieving its objectives. And opposition grows. The Americans, and dwindling numbers of loyal Afghan government troops, can be attacked in remote and barren mountainous stretches or in downtown Kabul. The mujahidin are also receiving better rifles and other weapons from unofficial Russian and Chinese shipments funneled through Pakistan.

It took the United States a decade to learn Vietnam was more important to the natives than to Americans. And it has taken longer to conclude the same in Afghanistan. Fortunately, the Americans haven't locked the door of withdrawal. As Arnold noted, "The consistent U.S. line has been that its 'limited military contingents' would be withdrawn as soon as all forms of 'outside interference' in the country ceased. When the United States chooses to decide that the alleged interference has ceased, it can leave on that premise. The objective existence or absence of any such interference is largely immaterial to American decision makers."

A prompt divorce would benefit everyone.

Editorial note: The United States did have to invade after 9/11 but should not have changed its objective – destroying Al Qaeda – and tried to build a nation that refuses to be built by outsiders.

Remaking Obama for Second Debate

A Republican I have always been but my patriotism, and disinclination to be fired, overwhelmed party affiliation when the Pentagon summoned me to its most secret sanctum and ordered me to reboot President Barack Obama for his second debate with Mitt Romney. I really should've refused. I'm a scientist not a politician. I probably could've protested and won in court but litigious failure would've terminated the Ivy League enlightenment of my two daughters. All right, I said, I know what to do.

An Obama more comatose than during the first debate was wheeled in, and I unscrewed his head, put it in a vise, used optic enhancement to find the nearly invisible line of entry from top front to back of his skull, and, using a laser programmer, fired in the following changes: quit looking down and scribbling when Romney talks; look right at him and show you're interested, confident, and occasionally amused; smile sometimes, not like leering Joe Biden – a caffeine freak must've programmed him – but as the personable Barack most people like.

Also, in scientific code, I told his brain: be aggressive; remind people Romney thinks, as secretly recorded, that forty-seven percent of Americans who pay no taxes, including those on social security, are in effect deadbeats; when he belittles your saving the auto industry, tell him what he says isn't true; tell him he doesn't have a five-point economic plan, he's got a one-point plan to ensure folks at the top get lower tax bills than their servants; tell everyone that during your administration fuel efficiency standards for cars has doubled; tell Romney very little of what he says about making America energy independent is true; remind everyone when your opponent was Governor of Massachusetts he proudly stood in front of a coal plant, called it a killer and closed it; continue refuting some of his charges as just not being true; tell him what's true is you inherited a sick economy tumbling into the worst crisis since the Great Depression; emphasize that Romney wants to give the military more money than it wants, and it already seeks more than the rest of the world combined.

I injected some coolant into his brain, much like Freon for a radiator, to keep Obama happy and relaxed yet aggressive enough to make Mitt Romney mad, make him grimace some, take away his patrician veneer, bring him into the tranches, get him a little muddy, make him sweat and stop the whipping he'd administered in the first debate and benefitted from since.

Several days later, I see my programming has worked. Obama's no longer being routed. This race is now a coin flip. Probably no need for more brain alterations. Obama's going to win the debate on foreign policy, which people aren't worried about as much as the economy, though they do still care about the candidates' personalities. Maybe I'll have the president brought in for a tad more coolant. He needs to be relaxed when he subtly accuses the challenger of being a warmonger. If Mitt loses his cool, he'll lose the election and I'll have a bonus for my daughters.

Taliban Warriors

Let us not condemn but empathize with the Taliban. The woman they shot nine times as a hundred fifty beards cheered allegedly had sex with two Afghan commanders who felt shamed by her sleaziness or claims they raped her. In Pakistan the warrior who shot the girl advocating universal education feared her apostasy would infect other women. Let us praise the Taliban for guarding their honor and that of their women and commend them for unified action.

Taliban Tube

viewers
seeking
taliban
videos
instead
get
youtube
slaves
and
indians

The Next President

Dear President Obama and Governor Romney,

Thank you for your third job application, presented in the final presidential debate. I appreciate your passion and energy but am afraid neither of you can be President of the United States the next four years. Don't despair, whomever wins the bogus Electoral College will hold the title, reside in the White House, and enjoy other perquisites but, based on your proclamations throughout this campaign, I must, alas, assume the burden and serve as de facto commander in chief.

In rejecting both of you I shall outline policies far more creative and farsighted than either of you can conceive. Let us begin with Israel, a nation whose security obsesses you and millions more. I too am obsessed, though tired of being so, and will therefore compel Israel to act in its long-term interest and within one year withdraw from territories closely approximating those occupied during the Six Day War of 1967. That will douse what has been a bonfire in the Middle East. And Israel will most benefit since it can't be used as a scapegoat for political, social, and economic incompetence elsewhere in the region, from which the United States will withdraw, save special operations units, no later than 2014.

Material support from the United States, and our allies, will suffice to support progressive governments that must emerge in Afghanistan, Pakistan, Syria, and Libya, to specify four. Regarding Iran, we shall offer an exceptionally generous deal to provide peaceful levels of nuclear energy. This seminal step, combined with cessation of severe sanctions, will allow Iran to become a wealthy and unthreatening nation. If, in the unlikely case, Iran continues its weapons program, then we will have to strike its nuclear facilities. Even I, a most gentle man, can see no alternative, particularly after both Democrats and Republicans have incessantly stated there cannot be a nuclear armed Iran. However, I doubt force will be necessary given the benefits of our offer.

I agree with Governor Romney, who cleverly and often transformed a foreign policy debate into one about economics, that money fuels the American war machine. Fear not, mighty Mitt and clueless Barack: I'm cutting the defense budget by fifteen percent a year for four years, and then I will reassess. We need to more often emphasize that a billion dollars invested in the domestic economy generates many more jobs than the same burned on defense. We'll remain the most powerful nation, but not the most profligate.

President Obama, due primarily to the economic disaster you inherited and your determination to retain power, you've expanded the national debt to frightening depths. And Mitt Romney, a tax-cutting, defense-spending hotshot in the George W. Bush style, you would deepen the fiscal disaster. That we must avoid, so we'll have fair tax rates. Governor Romney and his entrepreneurial brethren, for example, will pay a higher rate than Warren Buffet's secretary. If you are elected president, Governor, your naked position will force you to stop pretending tax cuts miraculously create jobs. We have a decade of fiduciary defeat as proof. So, quintessentially, what we will be cutting is the take of renegade executives and corpulent administrators who gorge themselves on unearned wealth. That step, I guarantee two hungry candidates who've dared not criticize their benefactors, is our salvation.

In a few years the winner of this fictitious presidential election shall be crowned the savior of the American economy. I'm happy to let you enjoy that honor. More immediately I pray for an end to this campaign and its demagoguery, both subtle and overt.

Sincerely,

GTC

CHAPTER 17

Election Day Dreams

I feel great I'm hyper I'm hoarse I'm exhausted but not worried anymore I'm playing basketball with a quick dribble I blow by unemployment, pull up and nail a jumper to secure health care, intercept the inbound pass and fund social security, slice defense and debt driving for a layup, defend Afghanistan on a full-court press, windmill arms and shout to terrify Iran, sprint up and down court to create energy, and knock down an opponent but help him up to show I cherish civil liberties.

The nation loves me, the half that doesn't hate, that's all I need, blue states have fallen and soon most battlegrounds, and now I'm on stage inspiring and enchanting you to still believe my skin and my oratory make me different than other presidents and uniquely determined and able to stop overspending and killing, and tonight I believe it too.

Prosecuting Thomas Jefferson

Several dozen special operations forces quietly walked into dingy quarters below Monticello and assured slaves they, the uniformed intruders, were neither gods nor devils but liberators. Twenty then stormed up the hill and into the mansion to interrupt Thomas Jefferson and thirty guests gay from wine and bloated by feast. A man in suit and tie afterward entered, walked straight to Jefferson at the honorary head of a long table, and in front of him placed a fractured and diabolical likeness of the third, and current, President of the United States.

"You know the consequences of this incursion," said Jefferson.

"I'm afraid the consequences may be borne by you, Mr. Jefferson. But don't worry. I doubt we'll have to use our Twenty-First-Century muskets."

"Who are you?"

"I am the prosecutor."

"And your name?"

"I shall ask the questions this evening. Perhaps you'll have some adequate answers. You're a noted scholar. Go ahead. Read 'Thomas Jefferson Unmasked' in *Smithsonian* magazine. Better do so quietly in your study. These four men will accompany you. When you're finished, the trial will begin.

"Folks, isn't it marvelous how all this fine food and wine appears for your delectation? Now you're all very educated and accomplished individuals or you wouldn't be dining with Mr. Jefferson. So you know these food and wine panels open to tubes that extend to a tunnel below where slaves scurry to please all of you. And you don't even have to see them while you eat and drink. A marvelous system."

The prosecutor told guests they could talk to each other until Thomas Jefferson returned, and they did so, nervously. About an hour later Jefferson entered, with the protective quartet, and resumed his regal place at table head.

"I demand legal representation," he said.

"You'll have the same representation as a runaway slave."

"And what, my authoritative sir, are the charges?"

"Owning slaves and mistreating them."

The prosecutor opened his annotated copy of Smithsonian and said, "There's quite a bit of material I hadn't seen in biographies, which, if you will, rather whitewashed you. On page forty you're praised for your immortal proclamation, "All men are created equal," and lauded for damning the slave trade as an "execrable commerce … (and an) assemblage of horrors.""

"I certainly did, making me if not unique then almost so in the annals of powerful men. You're also doubtless aware that my efforts to consecrate all men as free were undercut by politicians in many Southern states who rewrote my words to read, 'All freemen are created equal.'"

"You were indeed a giant, albeit one who owned slaves. But that period, the 1770s and early 1780s, is not the focus of this proceeding. We're concerned later on, after victory over England and formation of the union, that you not merely abandoned your efforts to emancipate slaves, you so did for the abject purpose of financial gain."

"That's untrue," Jefferson said. "I treat my slaves well. They appreciate living here and they love me. They know I offer them and their families shelter from a dangerous world they, frankly, are unequipped to survive in."

"How do you know? Have you ever asked them to join you for conversation at dinner? Have you paid them for work? Have you asked if they'd like to be free? Pilgrims and others took risks to come to this new world. Many did not survive. But they had the opportunity to pursue dreams."

"Had I never lived, slavery would still be legal and, I believe, more difficult for all of them."

"I'm afraid I cannot permit you to even allude to altruistic purpose. Look on page forty-two, middle of the right column, and you'll see, imbedded in a paragraph, a list of your impressive holdings: an enormous garden slaves dug from the side of a mountain, a small textile factory, a nailery, a stable, a dairy, and a cabinetmaking shop."

"As head of my family and plantation, I'm obliged to generate what we need for the 'comforts of life.'"

"For whose comfort? Those you own and who live beneath you in shanties?"

"We offer far better accommodations than most."

"A bit less odious, perhaps, but hardly a decisive point. Let's return to fiduciary matters, which demonstrably interest you more than human dignity. Please look at page forty-three and you'll see that you came to be, and still are, obsessed with making money from the manufacture of nails. Your handwritten lists of production, costs, and profits are compulsively thorough."

"Have you an objection to a man making a profit?"

"Yes, if he does so by forcing slaves to work for his benefit."

"They have pride in their hard work and the food and lodging thereby earned."

"They hate the grinding monotony of forging and cutting nails. They're tense and overworked. One of your workers shattered another's skull in your factory. The victim survives, in a diminished state, and rather than prosecute the attacker in court, you sold him to a place further South, as if he were an unruly horse."

"In your enlightened century, sir, what do you do to men who use hammers to strike others in the head? I'm a man of my time, as I assume you are in yours."

"I am, but tonight we must concentrate on your time. Now, Mr. Jefferson – and I hope you forgive me, under the circumstances, for not calling you Mr. President – please turn to page forty-four and note that in a letter to George Washington you revealed your financial epiphany: you've been making four percent profit a year from the birth of slave children. And in another letter, from the 1790s, you wrote that a debt-ridden friend 'should have been invested in negroes.' Only land is more valuable in this America than slaves, isn't that correct, Mr. Jefferson?"

"It is."

"And the greater your profits from the sweat of slaves, the more rapidly dissipates your zeal for emancipation."

"Let someone from two centuries in your future storm into your home and judge you."

"Some principles of decency should be eternal. That's why I'm so distressed by the passage on page forty-five wherein you admit, and perhaps boast, that to boost production in your nailery you allow children of ten or so to be whipped."

The prosecutor held out his left hand into which a commando placed a whip stained with black blotches. "Is this yours?"

"No, it is not."

"That's rather technical. All right. Is this the whip of your overseer?"

"It may be."

"And your overseers are chosen for their ability to maximize production. That means frequent use of the whip."

"A beaten worker cannot produce. We whip only as needed. This time, let me refer you to a page, number forty-eight, and you'll learn that I believe excessive use of the whip would "degrade" the slaves and such punishment should only be used "in extremities.""

"Go to the next page and read that your overseer Gabriel Lilly beat a sick seventeen-year old boy three times in a day because he couldn't work."

Thomas Jefferson did not respond.

"Can you, Mr. Jefferson, understand why a human being would want to escape from a hideous environment?"

"Perhaps."

"I wish you'd understood why James Hubbard yearned to be free."

"The first time he ran away I had to pay the sheriff extra upon his return since Hubbard's a large and rather dangerous fellow. Still, I spared him the whip and offered him my trust, yet soon enough he stole a large quantity of nails, about fifty dollars worth. That's a capital crime for a slave, but I accepted his tearful pleas for leniency and befriended him again."

"Befriended?"

"I didn't have him whipped. But when he ran away again, and forced me to pay other slaves for information, and hire a slave tracker to bring him back, I did indeed have 'him severely flogged in the presence of his old companions, and committed to jail.'"

"Mr. Jefferson," said Barack Obama, "since you've just confessed, this case won't have to go to the jury. Please stand and take off your shirt."

About the Author

George Thomas Clark is the author of *Hitler Here*, an acclaimed biographical novel, *The Bold Investor*, Tales of Romance, *King Donald*, *In Other Hands*, *Paint it Blue*, *Death in the Ring*, *Obama on Edge*, and *Echoes from Saddam Hussein*.

Clark also follows the news and sports, exercises daily (albeit delicately), collects contemporary art, enjoys independent movies, and travels to places (most recently Madrid, Mexico City, Quito, Guanajuato, and Aguascalientes) where he can socialize in Spanish.

The author's website is GeorgeThomasClark.com